Charles Robinson, William Brightly Rands

Lilliput Lyrics

Charles Robinson, William Brightly Rands

Lilliput Lyrics

ISBN/EAN: 9783744766371

Printed in Europe, USA, Canada, Australia, Japan

Cover: Foto ©Andreas Hilbeck / pixelio.de

More available books at **www.hansebooks.com**

LILLIPUT LYRICS

EDITED BY
R. BRIMLEY
JOHNSON.

BY W. B.
RANDS
ILLUSTRA
TED BY
CHAS. ROB
INSON.

JOHN LANE
THE BODLEY HEAD.
LONDON & NEW YORK. 1899

LILLIPUT LYRICS.

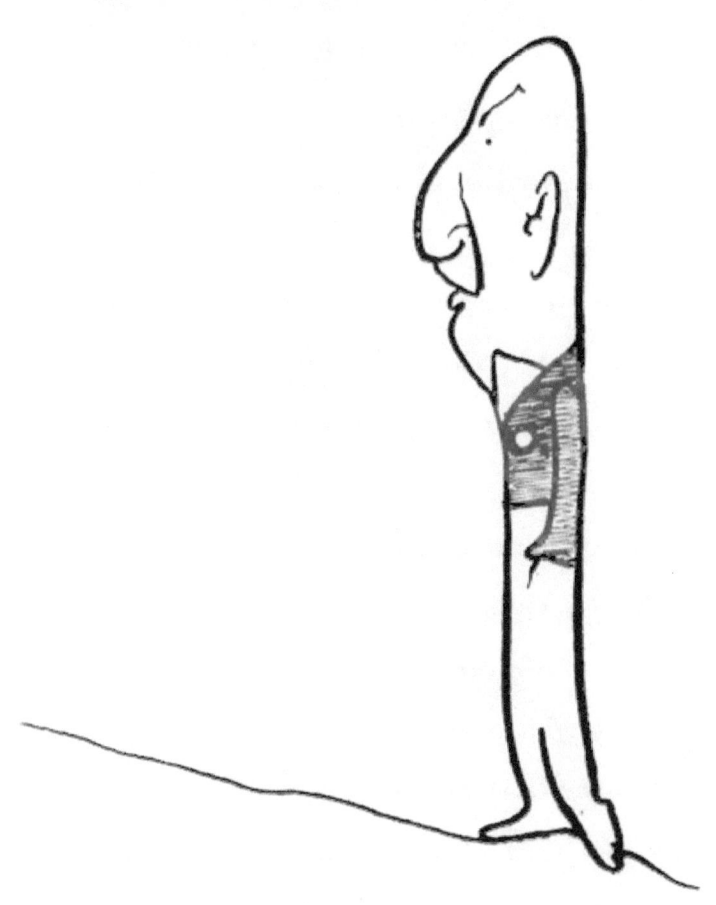

THE EDITOR'S NOTE

THE following verses have been selected from "Lilliput Levee," 1868, and from W. B. Rands' numerous contributions to magazines.* He wrote

* A portion of the Introductory Verses to "Lilliput Legends" is also included.

under many signatures, never enumerated; but— with the generous assistance of his son, Mr. Paul W. Rands, and his publisher, Mr. Alexander Strahan—I have been able to identify and examine all his work. Three poems are included, by permission, from the reprint of "Lilliput Lectures," which I lately edited for Mr. James Bowden. Messrs. Dalziel have allowed me to use one from "Hood's Comic Annual." All other rights belonged to Mr. Strahan, and have been transferred, with the full concurrence of Mr. P. W. Rands, to Mr. John Lane for this volume. Nothing has been included from "Innocent's Island," which we hope to reprint shortly with some of the "Lilliput Revels."

These are poems for children, with whom Rands was always at his best, and have been chosen in remembrance of their tastes and understandings. As many of them are printed from magazines and never received the author's final revision, I have occasionally edited the text, without scruple, by omitting weak lines or even altering a word.

R. B. J.

RAT-TAT ! the postman knocks !
This is the Lilliput letter-box.
A penny for your thoughts, my dear !
So said the Raven in Odin's ear.
Here comes a letter from Thing-a-my-Bob,
A letter from Ruth, a letter from Rob.
Rat-tat ! the postman knocks !
This is the Lilliput letter-box.

· CONTENTS

CONTENTS

12

CONTENTS

NONSENSE RHYMES

CONTENTS

Lyric

LILLIPUT LEVEE

WHERE does Pianofore Palace stand?
Right in the middle of Lilliput-land!
There the Queen eats bread-and-honey,
There the King counts up his money!

17

LILLIPUT LEVEE

Oh, the Glorious Revolution!
Oh, the Provisional Constitution!
Now that the children, clever bold folks,
Have turned the tables upon the Old Folks!

Easily the thing was done,
For the children were more than two to one;
Brave as lions, quick as foxes,
With hoards of wealth in their money-boxes!

They seized the keys, they patrolled the street,
They drove the policeman off his beat,
They built barricades, they stationed sentries—
You must give the word, when you come to the
      entries!

They dressed themselves in the Riflemen's clothes,
They had pea-shooters, they had arrows and bows,
So as to put resistance down—
Order reigns in Lilliput-town!

They made the baker bake hot rolls,
They made the wharfinger send in coals,
They made the butcher kill the calf,
They cut the telegraph-wires in half.

They went to the chemist's, and with their feet
They kicked the physic all down the street;
They went to the schoolroom and tore the books,
They munched the puffs at the pastrycook's.

LILLIPUT LEVEE

They sucked the jam, they lost the spoons,
They sent up several fire-balloons,
They let off crackers, they burnt a guy,
They piled a bonfire ever so high.

They offered a prize for the laziest boy,
And one for the most Magnificent toy;
They split or burnt the canes off'hand,
They made new laws in Lilliput-land.

Never do to-day what you can
Put off till to-morrow, one of them ran;
Late to bed and late to rise
Was another law which they did devise.

They passed a law to have always plenty
Of beautiful things: we shall mention twenty:
A magic lantern for all to see,
Rabbits to keep, and a Christmas-tree,

A boat, a house that went on wheels,
An organ to grind, and sherry at meals,
Drums and wheelbarrows, Roman candles,
Whips with whistles let into the handles,

A real live giant, a roc to fly,
A goat to tease, a copper to sky,
A garret of apples, a box of paints,
A saw and a hammer, and no complaints.

Nail up the door, slide down the stairs,
Saw off the legs of the parlour chairs—
That was the way in Lilliput-land,
The children having the upper hand.

They made the Old Folks come to school,
And in pinafores,—that was the rule,—
Saying, *Eener-deener-diner-duss,*
Kattler-wheeler-whiler-wuss ;

They made them learn all sorts of things
That nobody liked. They had catechisings ;
They kept them in, they sent them down
In class, in school, in Lilliput-town.

O but they gave them tit-for-tat !
Thick bread-and-butter, and all that ;
Stick-jaw pudding that tires your chin,
With the marmalade spread ever so thin !

They governed the clock in Lilliput-land,
They altered the hour or the minute-hand,
They made the day fast, they made the day slow,
Just as they wished the time to go.

They never waited for king or for cat ;
They never wiped their shoes on the mat ;
Their joy was great ; their joy was greater ;
They rode in the baby's perambulator !

LILLIPUT LEVEE

There was a Levee in Lilliput-town,
At Pinafore Palace. Smith and Brown,
Jones and Robinson had to attend—
All to whom they cards did send.

Every one rode in a cab to the door;
Every one came in a pinafore;
Lady and gentleman, rat-tat-tat,
Loud knock, proud knock, opera hat!

The place was covered with silver and gold,
The place was as full as it ever could hold;
The ladies kissed her Majesty's hand,
Such was the custom in Lilliput-land.

His Majesty knighted eight or ten,
Perhaps a score, of the gentlemen,
Some of them short and some of them tall—
Arise, Sir What's-a-name What-do-you-call!

Nuts and nutmeg (that's in the negus);
The bill of fare would perhaps fatigue us;
Forty-five fiddlers to play the fiddle;
Right foot, left foot, down the middle.

Conjuring tricks with the poker and tongs,
Riddles and forfeits, singing of songs;
One fat man, too fat by far,
Tried "Twinkle, twinkle, little star."

LILLIPUT LEVEE

His voice was gruff, his pinafore tight,
His wife said, "Mind, dear, sing it right,"
But he forgot, and said Fa-la-la!
The Queen of Lilliput's own papa!

She frowned, and ordered him up to bed:
He said he was sorry; she shook her head;
His clean shirt-front with his tears was stained—
But discipline had to be maintained.

The Constitution! The Law! The Crown!
Order reigns in Lilliput-town!
The Queen is Jill, and the King is John;
I trust the Government will get on.

I noticed, being a man of rhymes,
An advertisement in the *Lilliput Times* :—
"PINAFORE PALACE. This is to state
That the Court is in want of a Laureate.

" Nothing menial required.
Poets, willing to be hired,
May send in Specimens at once,
Care of the Chamberlain DOUBLEDUNCE."

Said I to myself Here's a chance for me
The Lilliput Laureate for to be!
And these are the Specimens I sent in
To Pinafore Palace. Shall I win?

LILLIPUT LEVEE

PUBLIC NOTICE.—*This is to state
That these are the specimens left at the gate
Of Pinafore Palace, exact to date,
In the hands of the porter, Curlypate,
Who sits in his plush on a chair of state,
By the gentleman who is a candidate*
    For the office of LILLIPUT LAUREATE.

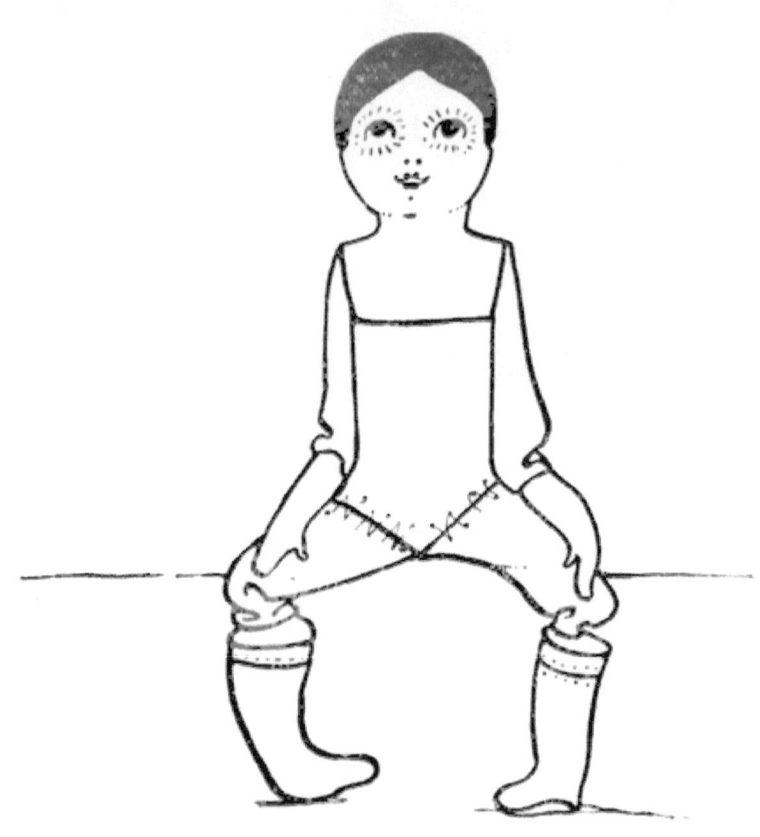

DOLL POEMS

I

THE PICTURE

THIS is her picture—Dolladine—
    The beautifullest doll that ever was seen!
Oh, what nosegays! Oh, what sashes!
Oh, what beautiful eyes and lashes!

Oh, what a precious perfect pet!
On each instep a pink rosette ;
Little blue shoes for her little blue tots ;
Elegant ribbons in bows and knots.

Her hair is powdered ; her arms are straight,
Only feel—she is quite a weight !
Her legs are limp, though ;—stand up, miss !—
What a beautiful buttoned-up mouth to kiss !

II

THE LOVE STORY

THIS is the doll with respect to whom
    A story is told that ends in gloom ;
For there was a sensitive little sir
Went out of his mind for love of her !

They pulled a wire, she moved her eye ;
They squeezed the bellows, they made her cry ;
But the boy could never be persuaded
That these were really things which *they* did.

" My Dolladine," he said, " has life ;
I love her, and she shall be my wife ;
Dainty delicate Dolladine,
The prettiest girl that ever was seen ! "

To give his passion a chance to cool,
They sent the lover to boarding-school.
But absence only made it worse—
He never learnt anything, prose or verse!

He drew her likeness on his slate;
His Grammar was in a *dreadful* state,
With Dolladine all over the edges,
And true-love knots, and vows, and pledges.

What was the consequence?—Doctor Whack
Begged of his parents to take him back.
When his condition, poor boy, was seen,
Too late, they sent for Dolladine.

And now he will never part with her:
He calls her lily, and rose, and myrrh,
Dolly-o'-diamonds, precious lamb,
Humming-bird, honey-pot, jewel, jam,

Darling, delicate-dear-delight,
Angel-o'-red, angel-o'-white,
Queen of beauty, and suchlike names;
In fact all manner of darts and flames!

Of course, while he keeps up this wooing
His education goes to ruin:
What are his prospects in future life,
With only a doll for his lawful wife?

It is feared his parents' hearts will break!
And there's one remark I wish to make:
I may be wrong, but it seems a pity
For a movable doll to be made too pretty.

An old-fashioned doll, that is not like nature,
Can never pass for a human creature;
It is in a doll that moves her eyes
That the danger of these misfortunes lies!

The lover's name must be suppressed
For obvious reasons. He lives out west,
And if I call him Pygmalion Pout,
I don't believe you will find him out!

III

DRESSING HER

THIS is the way we dress the Doll:—
　You may make her a shepherdess, the Doll,
If you give her a crook with a pastoral hook,
But this is the way we dress the Doll.

Chorus:　Bless the Doll, you may press the Doll,
　　　　But do not crumple and mess the Doll!
　　　　This is the way we dress the Doll.

27

First, you observe her little chemise,
As white as milk, with ruches of silk ;
And the little drawers that cover her knees,
As she sits or stands, with golden bands,
And lace in beautiful filagrees.

Chorus : Bless the Doll, you may press the Doll,
  But do not crumple or mess the Doll !
  This is the way we dress the Doll.

Now these are the bodies : she has two,
One of pink, with ruches of blue,
And sweet white lace ; be careful, do !
And one of green, with buttons of sheen,
Buttons and bands of gold, I mean,
With lace on the border in lovely order,
The most expensive we can afford her !

Chorus : Bless the Doll, you may press the Doll,
  But do not crumple or mess the Doll !
  This is the way we dress the Doll.

Then, with black at the border, jacket ;
And this—and this—she will not lack it ;
Skirts ? Why, there are skirts, of course,
And shoes and stockings we shall enforce,
With a proper bodice, in the proper place
(Stays that lace have had their days
And made their martyrs) ; likewise garters,
All entire. But our desire

Is to show you her night attire,
At least a part of it. Pray admire
This sweet white thing that she goes to bed in!
It's not the one that's made for her wedding;
That is special, a new design,
Made with a charm and a countersign,
Three times three and nine times nine:
These are only her usual clothes:
Look, *there's* a wardrobe! gracious knows
It's pretty enough, as far as it goes!

So you see the way we dress the Doll:
You might make her a shepherdess, the Doll,
If you gave her a crook with a pastoral hook,
With sheep, and a shed, and a shallow brook,
And all that, out of the poetry-book.

Chorus: Bless the Doll, you may press the Doll,
             But do not crumple and mess the Doll!
             This is the way we dress the Doll;
             If you had not seen, could you guess the
             Doll?

THE LITTLE DOLL'S HOUSE IN
ARCADY

THE boys and girls were exceeding gay,
  With billycock bonnets and curds and whey,
And I thought that I was in Arcady,
For the fringe of the forest was fair to see.

But the very first hayrick that I came to
Did turn to a Doll's House, fair and true;
I saw with my eyes where the same did sit,
And there was a rainbow over it.

The people inside were setting the platters,
The chairs and tables, and suchlike matters,
And making the beds and getting the tea:
But through a bow-window I saw the sea.

Up came a damsel: "Sir," she said,
"Will you walk with me by my garden bed?
Will you sit in my parlour by-and-by?"
"I will sit in your parlour, my dear," said I.

"Will you hear my starling gossip?" said she,
And now I felt sure it was Arcady;
But a starling never could do the rhyming
That very soon in my ears was chiming:—

"Jigglum-jogglum, Lilliputlandum,
Twopenny tiptop, sugaricandum,
Snip-snap snorum, hot-cross buns,
Conjugatorum, double-dunce.

"Fannyfold funnyface, fairy-tale,
Cat in a cockle-boat, wigglum-whale,
Dickory-dolphin, humpty-hoo,
Floppety-fluteykin, tootle-tum-too."

DOLL'S HOUSE IN ARCADY

Said I, "There may be a clown outside,
And a clown I never could yet abide,—
A picker and stealer, a clumsy joker,
Who stirs up his friends with a burning poker.

"But perhaps," said I, "I mistake the plan;
It may be the Punch-and-Judy man,
Or the other, that keeps the galante show
And the marionettes, for what I know."

Then I opened the window through thick and
    thin,
And in with a bounce came a Harlequin,
And very distinctly I heard a band
Strike up the dances of Lilliput Land.

To wonder at this I did incline,
"And where," said I, "is the Columbine—
Tip-toe twist-about, shimmer and shine,
Where is the beautiful Columbine?"

Then out from the curtains, all shimmer and
    shine,
With a rose-red sash came Columbine,
And Harlequin took her by the hand,
And they stepped it out in Lilliput Land;
Twirl about, whirl about, shimmer and shine,
O a rose-red sash had Columbine!

Then one of the folks who had set the tea
In Doll's House fashion, did climb my knee,
And he said, "Would you like, sir, to take a trip
With me? Have you seen my little ship?"

The ship, as he called it, was certainly small,
For the dot of a sailor could carry it all:
So both got in, and away went we,
Coasting the sea-board of Arcady.

Then I told a story, and he told one,
But they both got mixed before they were done;
And so did we, as the day grew dim,
And the child was myself, and myself was him.

But now it was getting time to land,
So I stepped into Fleet Street, and went up the
    Strand,
For I thought I should like to study the trade
They drive in toys at the Lowther Arcade.

And whom should I see, at a Doll's House door,
But the very same damsel I met before!
"I thought I should see you again," says she;
"And a few of my friends will be here to tea."

Then the Punch-and-Judy man came in,
And Columbine and the Harlequin,
The man that patters in front of the show,
And the children—and how their tongues did go!

But what makes the place so sweet? thought I,
As scents of the heather and furze went by,
And with them a whiff of the rolling sea;—
And then I remembered Arcady,
As the party were tittering over the tea.

THE PEDLAR'S CARAVAN

I WISH I lived in a caravan,
  With a horse to drive, like a pedlar-man!
Where he comes from nobody knows,
Or where he goes to, but on he goes!

His caravan has windows two,
And a chimney of tin, that the smoke comes
  through;
He has a wife, with a baby brown,
And they go riding from town to town.

THE PEDLAR'S CARAVAN

Chairs to mend, and delf to sell!
He clashes the basins like a bell;
Tea-trays, baskets ranged in order,
Plates, with alphabets round the border!

The roads are brown, and the sea is green,
But his house is like a bathing-machine;
The world is round, and he can ride,
Rumble and slash, to the other side!

With the pedlar-man I should like to roam,
And write a book when I came home;
All the people would read my book,
Just like the Travels of Captain Cook!

THE FIRST TOOTH

THERE once was a wood, and a very thick
    wood,
So thick that to walk was as much as you could;
But a sunbeam got in, and the trees understood.

THE FIRST TOOTH

I went to this wood, at the end of the snows,
And as I was walking I saw a primrose;
Only one! Shall I show you the place where it
    grows?

There once was a house, and a very dark house,
As dark, I believe, as the hole of a mouse,
Or a tree in my wood, at the thick of the
    boughs.

I went to this house, and I searched it aright,
I opened the chambers, and I found a light;
Only one! Shall I show you this little lamp
    bright?

There once was a cave, and this very dark cave
One day took a gift from an incoming wave;
And I made up my mind to know what the sea
    gave.

I took a lit torch, I walked round the ness
When the water was lowest; and in a recess
In my cave was a jewel. Will nobody guess?

O there was a baby, he sat on my knee,
With a pearl in his mouth that was precious to
    me,
His little dark mouth like my cave of the sea!

THE FIRST TOOTH

I said to my heart, " And my jewel is bright!
He blooms like a primrose! He shines like a
    light!"
Put your hand in his mouth! Do you feel? He can
    bite !

PRAISE AND LOVE

TELL me, Praise, and tell me, Love,
What you both are thinking of?

PRAISE AND LOVE

"Oh, we think," said Love, said Praise,
"Now of children and their ways."

Give me of your cup to drink,
Praise, and tell me all you think.

"Oh, I think of crowns of gold
For the clever and the bold."

Then I turned to Love, and said,—
Love was glowing heavenly-red,—

Give me of your cup to drink,
Love, and tell me all you think.

Let me taste your bitter-sweet;
Who are those that kiss your feet?

Love looked up—I read her eyes—
They were stars and they were skies.

Clinging to her garment's hem,
Smiling as I looked at them,

There were children scarred and halt,
Children weeping for a fault;

PRAISE AND LOVE

Those who scarcely dared to raise
Doubtful eyes to smiling Praise.

Love looked round, and Praise and Pride
Brought their glad ones to her side.

"Yea, these too," she said or sang,
And the world with music rang.

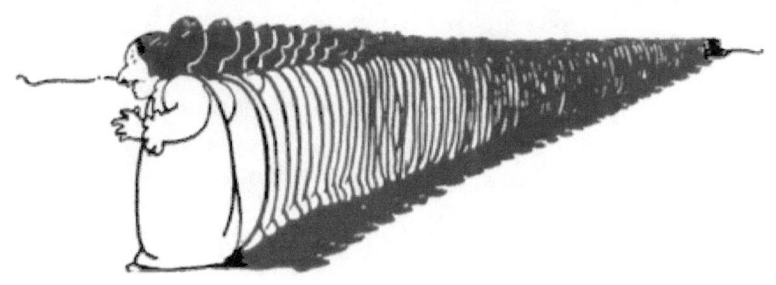

TWO PICTURES

I

THERE was a little fellow
　　Who lived across the sea,
His hair was brown and yellow
　　As any honey-bee.
Sometimes he was the smartest
　　Of warriors in the van;
He was a Bonapartist,
　　And a Republican.

A fort of cards he builded,
  Though now and then they slid;
With ammunition filled it,
  Or made believe he did;
And when the fort was wrought up,
  This little man amain
His big artillery brought up,
  And blew it down again!

II

This little Bonapartist,
  Or, say, Republican,
Would sometimes play the artist,—
  The busy little man!
Sometimes he was untidy,
  Though often he was smart;
He thought that he was mighty
  In many kinds of Art.
He sat like any fixture,
  The drawing-board before;
And, oh, to see the mixture
  Of colours on the floor!
Such was this little fellow,
  Who lived across the sea,
Whose hair was brown and yellow,
  Just like a honey-bee.

III

Seven-and-seventy mothers,
　This side of the sea,
Said, "We know some others
　Quite as nice as he!"
Seven-and-seventy brothers
　Said, "And so do we!"
Seven-and-seventy sisters,
　Hearing this acclaim,
Said to those young misters,
　"We think just the same."

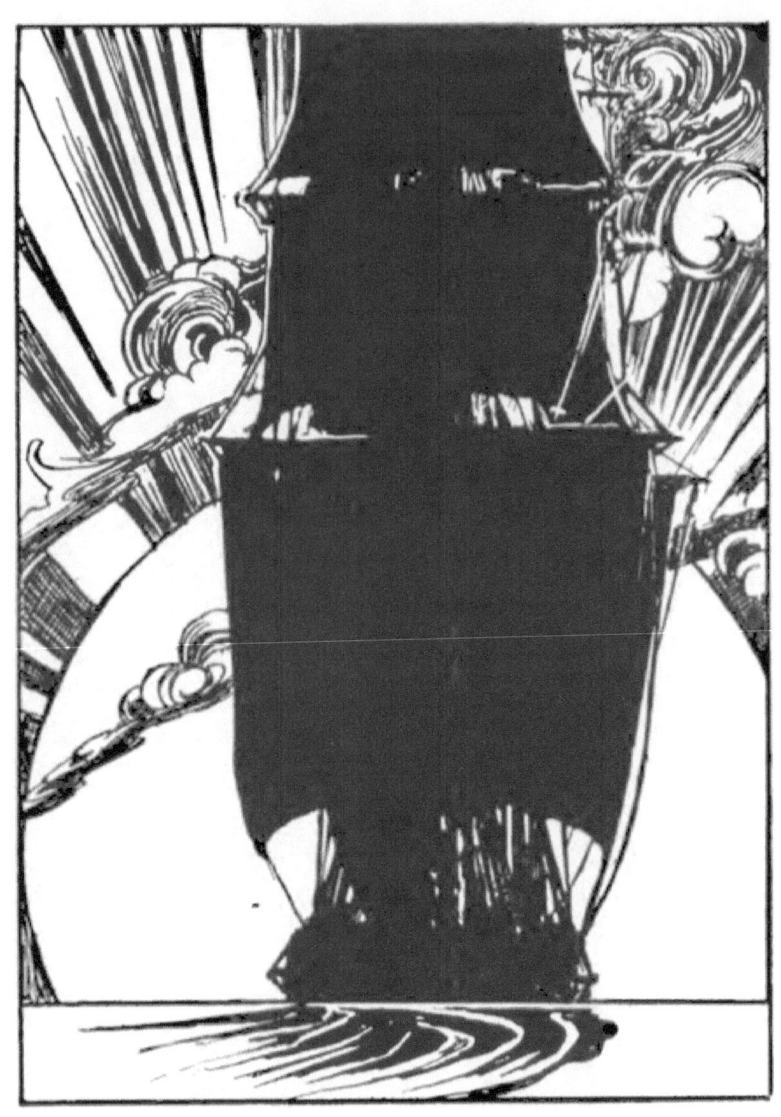

THE SHIP THAT SAILED INTO THE SUN

THEY said my brother's ship went down,
  Down into the sea,

THE SHIP THAT SAILED INTO THE SUN

Because a storm came on to drown
  The biggest ships that be;
But I saw the ship, when he went away;
  I saw it pass, and pass;
The tide was low, I went out to play,
  The sea was all like glass;
The ship sailed straight into the sun,
  Half of a ball of gold—
Onward it went till it touched the sun—
  I saw the ship take hold!

But soon I saw them both no more,
  The sun and the ship together,
For the wind began to hoot and to roar,
  And there was stormy weather.
Yet every day the golden ball
  Rests on the edge of the sky;
The sun it is, with the ship and all,
For the ship sailed into the golden ball
  Across the edge of the sky.

THE YOUNG EXILE

L ITTLE Boy
 From Savoy,
With the slouch-sandalled feet,
 With the pipe in your hand,
 To play on, as you stand
In the long, stony, stupid, stumbling street;

THE YOUNG EXILE

I heard a noise just now,
And I got up from my desk,
    Saying, "What can be the row?"
    For the dogs went bow-wow,
    And I-cannot-tell-you-how
Went your music; and the whole thing was
            grotesque.
Then I saw you, picturesque,
        In the weather,
        With a feather
In your rough wide-awake,
        And a bowl,
        Poor young soul!
In your hand for the coppers you might take;
        And the handsome face you had,
        Little lad,
    Olive skin of the South,
    Large eyes and well-set mouth,
I admired very much, yes, I did;
    And I wished you back again
    To your dear native plain
On the loose with a marmot or a kid;
With your father, and a bag full of money,
    In a cottage all your own
    Pretty much got up of stone,
        And with flocks
        In the rocks
    At your call, and the maids,
    Blue-kirtled, in the shades,
And a score of beehives very full of honey!

THE COMING STORM

THE tree-tops rustle, the tree-tops wave,
   They hustle, they bustle ; and, down in a cave,
The winds are murmuring, ready to rave.

The skies are dimming ; the birds fly low,
Skimming and swimming, their wings are slow ;
They float, they are carried, they scarcely go.

The dead leaves hurry ; the waters, too,
Flurry and scurry ; as if they knew
A storm was at hand ; the smoke is blue.

THE DISCONTENTED YEW-TREE

A DARK-GREEN prickly yew one night
    Peeped round on the trees of the forest,
And said, "*Their* leaves are smooth and bright,
    My lot is the worst and poorest:

I wish I had golden leaves," said the yew;
    And lo, when the morning came,
He found his wish had come suddenly true,
    For his branches were all aflame.

Now, by came a Jew, with a bag on his back,
  Who cried, " I'll be rich to-day ! "
He stripped the boughs, and, filling his sack
  With the yellow leaves, walked away !

The yew was as vexed as a tree could be,
  And grieved as a yew-tree grieves,
And sighed, " If Heaven would but pity me,
  And grant me crystal leaves ! "

Then crystal leaves crept over the boughs ;
  Said the yew, " Now am I not gay ? "
But a hailstorm hurricane soon arose
  And broke every leaf away !

So he mended his wish yet once again,—
  " Of my pride I do now repent ;
Give me fresh green leaves, quite smooth and
    plain,
  And I will be content."

In the morning he woke in smooth green leaf,
  Saying, " This is a sensible plan ;
The storm will not bring my beauty to grief,
  Or the greediness of man."

But the world has goats as well as men,
  And one came snuffing past,
Which ate of the green leaves a million and ten,
  Not having broken his fast.

O then the yew-tree groaned aloud,
  "What folly was mine, alack!
I was discontented, and I was proud—
  O give me my old leaves back!"

So, when daylight broke, he was dark, dark
    green,
  And prickly as before!—
The other trees mocked, "Such a sight to be
    seen!
  To be near him makes one sore!"
The south wind whispered his leaves between,
  "Be thankful, and change no more!

"The thing you are is always the thing
  That you had better be"—
But the north wind said, with a gallant fling,
  "The foolish, weak yew-tree!

"What if he blundered twice or thrice?
  There's a turn to the longest lane;
And everything must have its price—
  Poor faulterer, try again!"

THE LITTLE BROTHER

L ITTLE brother in a cot,
    Baby, baby!
Shall he have a pleasant lot?
    Maybe, maybe!

Little brother in a nap,
    Baby, baby!
Bless his tiny little cap,
    Noise far away be!

With a rattle in his hand,
    Baby, baby!
Dreaming—who can understand
    Dreams like this, what they be?

When he wakes kiss him twice,
    Then talk and gay be;
Little cheeks soft and nice,
    Baby, baby!

Pretty little pouting boy,
    Baby, baby!
Let his life, with sweet and toy,
    Pleasure all and play be.

Seven white angels watching here,
    Baby, baby!
Pray be kind to baby dear,
    Pray be, pray be!

Little brother in a cot,
    Baby, baby!
His shall be a pleasant lot—
    Must, not may be!

CUCKOO IN THE PEAR-TREE

THE Cuckoo sat in the old pear-tree.
                           Cuckoo!
Raining or snowing, nought cared he.
                           Cuckoo!
Cuckoo, cuckoo, nought cared he.

CUCKOO IN THE PEAR-TREE

The Cuckoo flew over a housetop nigh.
                Cuckoo !
"Dear, are you at home, for here am I?
                Cuckoo !
    Cuckoo, cuckoo, here am I."

"I dare not open the door to you.
                Cuckoo !
Perhaps you are not the right cuckoo?
                Cuckoo !
    Cuckoo, cuckoo, the right Cuckoo !"

"I am the right Cuckoo, the proper one.
                Cuckoo !
For I am my father's only son,
                Cuckoo !
    Cuckoo, cuckoo, his only son."

"If you are your father's only son—
                Cuckoo !
    The bobbin pull tightly,
    Come through the door lightly—
                Cuckoo !

If you are your father's only son—
                Cuckoo !
It must be you, the only one—
    Cuckoo, cuckoo, my own Cuckoo !
                Cuckoo !"

MADCAP

SWIFT, lithe, plastical;
    High-fantastical
In feats gymnastical;
Enthusiastical;

She is a glorious
Romp; victorious;
Is uproarious
Too censorious?

She is a mighty,
Elfy, spritey,
Highty-tighty
Ma'mselle Flighty.

MADCAP

The gayest wench, if
Her mood's extensive ;
But full of sense, if
Her mood is pensive.

What resolution
In execution !
'O mum," says Susan,
"She is a Rooshian !"

But when she's graver
No girl is braver
In her behaviour,
As I'm a shaver!

Bid Mystery pack again!
With sudden tack again,
My Romp is back again,
Madcap, clack again !

When I am priming
Myself for rhyming
Of Jove or Hymen,
That girl is climbing,

Athletic, able,
The chairs, the table,
An admirable
Gymnastic Babel!

MADCAP

It makes me shiver
In lungs and liver,
To look! However,
Three cheers I give her.

THE BEWITCHED TOYS;

OR,

QUEEN MAB IN CHILD-WORLD.

I

HERE comes Queen Mab in her coach-and-
six!
Look out for mischievous fairy tricks!

63

THE BEWITCHED TOYS

Look out, good girls! Look out, brave boys!
I know she comes to bewitch your toys!
Hither she floats, like the down of a thistle!—
So mind the pegtop; and mind the hoop;
Bring down the kite with a sudden swoop;
Hide the popgun; and plug up the whistle;
But don't say Dolly's a-bed with the croup:
For, if you tell her a fib, my dear,
She'll fasten the door-key to your ear!

II

Then the Kite went flying up to the Moon,
   And the Man with the Sticks, who lives up
     there,
Kick'd it through with his clouted shoon,
   And the tail hung dangling down in the air.

But Harry wouldn't let go the string,
   Although it nearly broke with the strain;
Said he: "Well, this is a comical thing,
   But the kite is mine, and I'll have it again!"

"Now whistle three times," cried cunning Nell,
   "And over your shoulder throw your shoe,
And pull once more, and say this spell:
   FUSTUMFUNNIDOSTANTARABOO!"

64

But Harry made a mistake in the charm,
   Saying, "FUSTUMFUNNIDOSTANTABOORACK !"
And a dreadful pain went all up his arm,
   And he fell down, shouting, right on his back.

Then Nell took hold, and pulled the string,
   And the kite came down, all safe and sound,
And a piece of the moon away did bring,
   Which you may have for a silver pound!

III

Said Thomas, with the round straw hat,
   " My popgun bring to me,
And hey ! to shoot the Tabby Cat
   Up in the Cherry-tree!

" Last night she stole my supper all,—
   She must be better taught;
And I shall make her caterwaul
   'I'm sorry,' as she ought."

Then Thomas, taking hasty aim
   At Tabby on the bough,
Hit Tabby's mistress, an old Dame
   Who had a Brindled Cow.

The Brindled Cow could not abide
   To see her mistress struck,
And after trembling Thomas hied,—
   Said he, "It's just my luck!"

She tossed him once, she tossed him twice,
   When Tabby at her flew,
Saying, "Tom, your custard was so nice
   That I will fight for you."

The old Dame flung the pellet back,
   And, when Tom picked it up,
He cried, "The pellet has turned, good lack!
   To a custard in a cup!"

And so it had! The Brindled Cow,
   The Dame, and Tabby Cat
Were much surprised. "It's strange, I vow,"
   Said Tom in the round hat.

But nothing came amiss to him;
   He ate the custard clean—
There was a brown mark round the rim
   To show where it had been.

IV

"Pegtop, pegtop—fast asleep!
Pray, how long do you mean to keep

Humming and droning and spinning away?
Do you mean to keep on all the day?
Ten minutes have passed since your nap was
  begun;
Pegtop, when will your nap be done?

" Forty winks, forty, and forty more!
You never slept so long before;
This is a pretty sleep to take!
Boxer, Boxer, yawn and wake!"

Then said Marian, "Never fear;
Dolly's nightcap, Richard dear,
Put on Boxer—perhaps he thinks
He would like forty times forty winks!

Three o'clock, four o'clock, all day long
Richard's pegtop hummed so strong,
Hummed away and would not stop—
Dick had to buy another top!
For though this Boxer was certainly clever,
Who wants a pegtop to hum for ever?

All the Queen's horses and all the Queen's men
Couldn't get Boxer to wake again;
They made him a house, and put him in;
The people came to see Boxer spin;
"A penny apiece," said Dick, "and cheap,
To see my Pegtop's wonderful sleep!"

V

Kate had quarrelled and would not speak
    To Cousin John,
Who, trying to kiss her on the cheek,
    With her bonnet on,
Had crumpled her bonnet at the border,
And put the trimming in disorder.

"Pray let me kiss you, Katy dear,"
    Said John so gay.
"Now, Master John," said Kate severe,
    "Please get away!
And if you don't, I only hope
You'll get hit with my skipping-rope!"

    Skip, skip,
    Never trip;
    Round and round!
    "Does it touch the ground?
Don't I skip well?" said sulky Kate;
    But, oh, at last
    Her feet stuck fast—
    Her pretty feet,
    So small and neat,
Were glued by magic to the skipping-cord,
Which turned into a Swing! And then my lord
Johnny said, "This is fine, upon my word!"

THE BEWITCHED TOYS

Backwards and forwards Katy swung ;—
To the magic rope, which by nothing hung,
Frightened out of her breath she clung—
An apple for the Queen, and a pear for the
   King !
Wasn't that a wonderful swing ?
It kept on going like anything !

"John !" said Katy, turning faint,
And the colour of white paint,
"Save me from this dreadful swing !"
Then our Johnny made a spring
Up to Kate, and held her tight,
And kissed her twice, with all his might,
Which stopped the magic swing ; and Katy then
Said, "Thank you, Jack !" and kissed him back
   again.

VI

Then the Children all said, "She spoils our play:
We must really get Queen Mab away ;
She mustn't bewitch our Toys too much.
Who will speak to her ? Does she talk Dutch ?
John knows Magic, and Greek, and such ;
No one than John can be cleverer—
Perhaps he knows how to get rid of her !"

VII

Six White Mice, with harness on,
What do you think of Cousin John,
    Who taught them so,
    And made them go?—
Six white mice, with harness on!

A wee coach, gilt like the Lord Mayor's own!
Made by Cousin John alone,
    Bright and gay,—
    On a Lord Mayor's Day
Just such a coach is the Lord Mayor's own!

Marian's Doll come out for a ride,
Dressed like a queen in pomp and pride:
    The six wee mice,
    That trot so nice,
Draw Marian's Doll come out for a ride!

Every mouse had a silver bell
Round its neck, as I've heard tell;
    Tinkle tink!—
    But who would think
Of a harnessed mouse, with a silver bell?

THE BEWITCHED TOYS

"What can six white mice intend?"
Thought Queen Mab, with her hair on end—
　　"And silver bells,
　　And what-not-else—
What can six white mice intend?

"When was such a procession seen?
It frightens me, as I'm a Queen!"
　　So she stopped her tricks,
　　And her coach-and-six
Drove away with the Fairy Queen.

THE NEW WORLD

I SAW a new world in my dream,
   Where all the folks alike did seem;
There was no Child, there was no Mother,
There was no Change, there was no Other,

For everything was Same, the Same;
There was no praise, there was no blame;
There was neither Need nor Help for it;
There was nothing fitting, or unfit.

Nobody laughed, nobody wept;
None grew weary, and so none slept;
There was nobody born, and nobody wed;
This world was a world of the living-dead.

I longed to hear the Time-Clock strike
In the world where the people were all alike;
I hated Same, I hated For-Ever,
I longed to say Neither, or even Never.

I longed to mend, I longed to make,
I longed to give, I longed to take,
I longed for a change, whatever came after,
I longed for crying, I longed for laughter.

At last I heard the Time-Clock boom,
And woke from my dream in my little room;
With a smile on her lips my mother was nigh,
And I heard the Baby crow and cry.

And I thought to myself,—How nice it is
For me to live in a world like this,
Where things can happen, and clocks can strike,
And none of the people are made alike;

THE NEW WORLD

Where Love wants this, and Pain wants that,
And all our hearts want Tit for Tat
In the jumbles we make with our heads and our
  hands,
In a world that nobody understands,
But with work, and hope, and the right to call
Upon Him who sees it and knows us all.

LINA AND HER LAMB

I

THIS is Lina, with her lamb,
   Lina and her lamb together,
In the pleasant, flowery weather.
"What a happy lamb I am!"—
That is what the lamb would say
   If the lamb could only speak—
   "Lina loves me all the week;
   Lina loves me night and day;
   Lina loves me all the hours;
   Lina goes to gather flowers;
Lina knows them, Lina finds them;
Lina takes the flowers, and binds them
   In a necklace for her lamb!"—
   Happy Lina, happy lamb!
Lina and her lamb together,
In the pleasant flowery weather.

LINA AND HER LAMB

II

This is Lina with her lamb,
   Lina and her lamb together,
   In the snowy winter weather;
" What a happy lamb I am ! "
That is what the lamb would say
If the lamb could only speak—
   " Lina loves me, Lina heeds me,
   Lina carries me, and feeds me ! "
Happy Lina, happy lamb !
Lina and her lamb together,
In the freezing winter weather.

THE BOY THAT LOVES A BABY

GOOD MORROW, Little Stranger,
　　Good morrow, Baby dear!
Good morrow, too, Mrs. Grainger,
　And what do you do here?
With your boxes, caps, and cap-strings,
Drowsy, hazard-hap things,
　And love of good cheer?

I'm a little boy that goes, ma'am,
　Straight to the point;
You said that my nose, ma'am,
　Would soon be out of joint;
But my nose keeps its place, ma'am—
The middle of my face, ma'am;
It is a nose of grace, ma'am—
　Aroint thee, aroint!

78

THE BOY THAT LOVES A BABY

Good morrow, Little Stranger,
  A girl, or a boy ?
Good morrow, Mrs. Grainger—
  Where are you, ma'am ?—ahoy !
Here's all things in their proper place,
  And people likewise,
The laundry-maid in the copper-place,
  The skylark in the skies !
Here's love for Mamma,
And love for Papa ;
Here's a penny for a scavenger,
And a bag for the blooming lavender,
  And a rope for Don't Care,
And a kiss for the little Baby,
And one for a pretty lady
  With a diamond in her hair !

HAROLD AND ALICE;

OR,

THE REFORMED GIANT

I

THE Giant sat on a rock up high,
 With the wind in his shaggy hair;
And he said, "I have drained the dairies dry,
 And stripped the orchards bare;

" I have eaten the sheep, with the wool on their
backs,"
(A nasty giant was he,)
" The eggs and the shells, the honey, the wax,
The fowls, and the cock-turkéy;

HAROLD AND ALICE

" And now I think I could eat a score
  Of babies so plump and small ;
And if, after that, I should want any more,
  Their brothers and sisters and all.

" To-morrow I'll do it. Ha! what was that ? "
  Said he, for a sound he heard ;
" Was it fluttering owl or pattering rat,
  Or bough to the breeze that stirred ? "

Oh, it was neither rat nor owl,
  Giant! nor shaking leaf ;
Young Harold has heard your scheme so foul,
  And it may come to grief !

One thing which you ate has escaped your mind,—
  Young Harold his guinea-pig dear ;
And he has crept up to try and find
  His pet, and he shakes with fear ;

He has hid himself in a corner, you know,
  To listen and look about ;
And if to the village to-morrow you go,
  You may find the babes gone out !

83

II

Now, when to the village came Harold back
  And told his tale so wild,
Then every mother she cried, "Good lack!
  My child! preserve my child!"

And every father took his sword
  And sharpened it on a stone;
But little Harold said never a word,
  Having a plan of his own.

He laid six harrows outside the stile
  That led to the village green,
Then on them a little hay did pile,
  For the prongs not to be seen.

A toothsome sucking-pig he slew,
  And thereby did it lay;
For why? Because young Harold knew
  The Giant would pass that way.

Then he went in and said his prayers,—
  Not to lie down to sleep;
But at his window up the stairs
  A watch all night did keep,

Till the little stars all went pale to bed,
  Because the sun was out,
And the sky in the east grew dapple-red,
  And the little birds chirped about.

III

Now, all the village was early awake,
  And, with short space to pray,
Their preparations they did make,
  To bear the babes away.

The horses were being buckled in,—
  The little ones looked for a ride,—
When on came the Giant, as ugly as Sin,
  With a terrible six-yard stride.

Then every woman and every child
  To scream aloud began;
Young Harold up at his watch-tower smiled,
  And his sword drew every man;

For now the Giant, fierce and big,
  Came near to the stile by the green,
But when he saw that luscious pig
  His lips grew wet between!

Now, left foot, right foot, step it again,
  He trod on——the harrow spikes!
And how he raged and roared with pain
  He may describe who likes.

At last he fell, and as he lay
  Loud bellowing on the ground,
The stalwart men of the village, they
  With drawn swords danced around.

"O spare my life, I you entreat!
  I will be a Giant good!
O take out those thorns that prick my feet,
  Which now are bathed in blood!"

Then the little village maids did feel
  For this Giant so shaggy-haired,
And to their parents they did kneel,
  Saying, "Let his life be spared!"

His bleeding wounds the maids did bind;
  They framed a litter strong
With all the hurdles they could find;
  Six horses drew him along;

And all the way to his castle rude
  Up high in the piny rocks,
He promised to be a Giant good---
  The cruel, crafty fox!

IV

"O mother, lend me your largest tub!"---
  "Why, daughter? tell me quick!"---
"O mother, to make a syllabub
  For the Giant who is so sick."

Now in fever-fit the Giant lay,
  From the pain in his wounded feet,
And hoping soon would come the day
  When he might the babies eat.

"O mother, dress me in white, I beg,
  With flowers and pretty gear;
For Mary and Madge, and Jess and Peg,
  And all my playmates dear,

" We go to the Giant's this afternoon,
    To carry him something nice,—
A custard three times as big as the moon,
    With sugar and wine and spice."

" O daughter, your father shall go with you;
    Suppose the Giant is well,
And eats you up, what shall we do?"
    Then her thought did Alice tell :—

" No, mother dear; we go alone,
    And Heaven for us will care;
If the Giant bad has a heart of stone,
    We will soften it with prayer !"

Now, when the Giant saw these maids,
    Drest all in white, draw near,
He twitched his monstrous shoulder-blades,
    And dropped an honest tear !

" Dear Giant, a syllabub nice we bring,
    Pray let us tuck you in !"
The Giant said, "Sweet innocent thing !
    "Oh, I am a lump of sin !

" Go home, and say to the man of prayer
    To make the church-door wide,
For I next Sunday will be there,
    And kneel, dears, at your side.

"Tell brave young Harold I forgive
  Him for the harrow-spikes;
And I will do, please Heaven I live,
  What penance the prayer-man likes.

"Set down, my dears, the syllabub,
  And as I better feel,
I'll try and eat a fox's cub
  At my next mid-day meal;

"And all my life the village I'll keep
  From harmful vermin free;
But never more will eat up the sheep,
  The honey, or cock-turkéy!"

V

Now Sunday came, and in the aisle
  Did kneel the Giant tall;
The priest could not forbear a smile,
  The church it looked so small!

And, as the Giant walked away,
  He knocked off the roof with his head;
But he quarried stones on the following day,
  To build another instead.

And it was high and broad and long,
  And a hundred years it stood,
To tell of the Giant so cruel and strong
  That kindness had made good.

And when Harold and Alice were married there,
  A handsome sight was seen;
For the bridegroom was brave, and the bride was
    fair—
    LONG LIVE OUR GRACIOUS QUEEN!

PRINCE PHILIBERT

OH, who loves Prince Philibert?
　　Who but myself?
His foot's in the stirrup;
　His book's on the shelf;

PRINCE PHILIBERT

His dapple-grey Dobbin
  Attends to his whip,
And rocks up and down
  On the floor like a ship.

I went to the pond with him,
  Just like the sea,
To swim his three-decker
  That's named after me;
His cheeks were like roses;
  He knew all the rocks;
He looks like a sailor
  In grey knickerbocks.

Oh, where is the keepsake
  I gave you, my prince?
I keep yours in a drawer
  That smells of a quince:
So how can I lose it?
  But you, giddy thing!
Keep mine in your pocket,
  Mixed up with some string.

Remember the riddle
  I told you last week!
And how I forgave you
  That scratch on the cheek!

PRINCE PHILIBERT

You could not have helped it,—
  You never would strike,
Intending to do it,
  The girl that you like!

You call me Miss Stupid,
  You call me Miss Prue;
But how do you like me
  In crimson and blue?
We go partners in findings,
  And money, and that,
You help me in ciphering;
  Look at my hat!

I love you, Prince Philibert!
  Who but myself?
With your foot in the stirrup,
  Your book on the shelf!
We call you a prince, John,
  But oh, when you crack
The nuts we go halves in,
  You're my Filbert Jack!

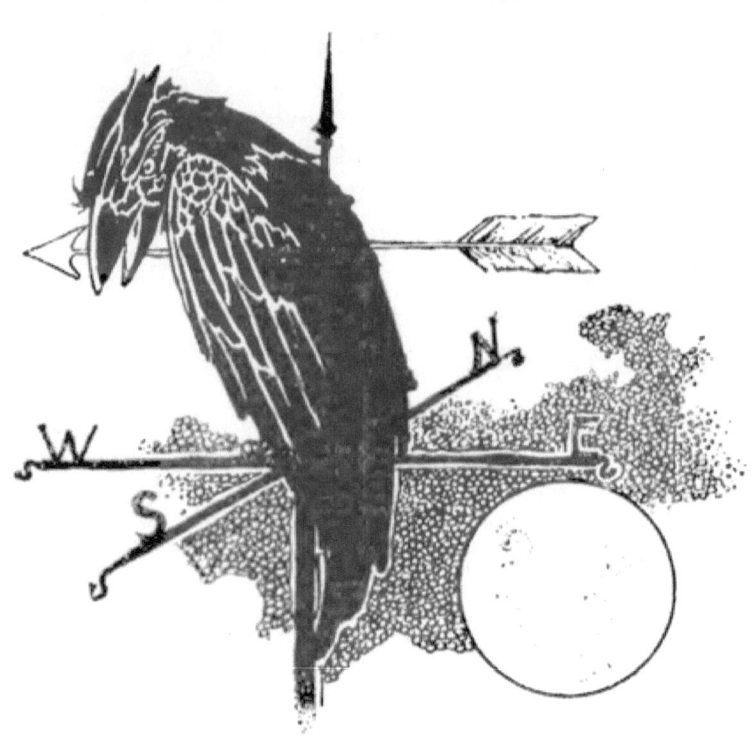

GOLD-BOY AND GREEN-GIRL

THERE was a little jackdaw
    Lived on a vane;
He was a very black daw,
    Shiny in the rain.

94

GOLD-BOY AND GREEN-GIRL

There was a boy in gold;
    There was a girl in green;
The lad was very bold;
    The maid was more serene.

There was a little church;
    It had a little steeple;
The jackdaw on his perch
    Cawed at the people.

This little golden boy
    And green damosel
Did make it their employ
    Their loves for to tell.

And early in the morning,
    It came into their head
Themselves to be adorning
    And go for to be wed.

The girl in green did stammer
    At saying *I take thee;*
Gaffer said, and Gammer,
    "What a pair they be!"

The yellow boy was bolder,
    And spoke up like a king,
As if he had been older—
    Hark, the bells ring!

GOLD-BOY AND GREEN-GIRL

In pops the jackdaw
At the belfry-door;
"Caw!" says the jackdaw,
"One peal more!"

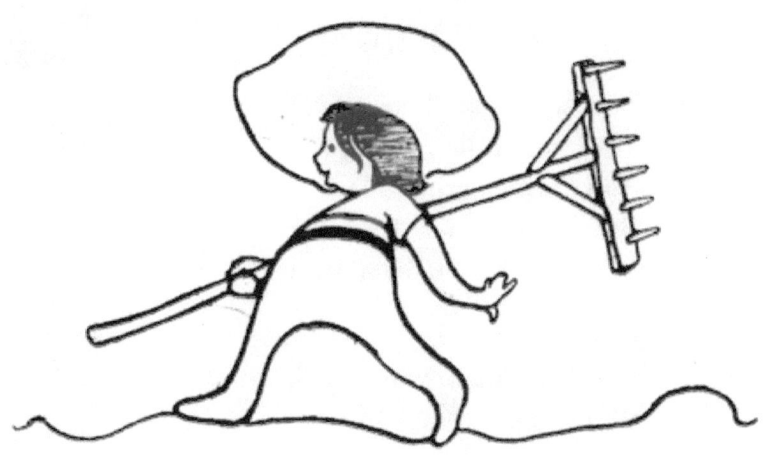

AT HARVEST-TIME

THE tawny sheaves of wheat
    Are standing on their feet,
They cuddle together,
They huddle together,
They laugh out bold,
Their tassels of gold
They toss up together;
They gossip together
In the harvest weather;
And what may the thing they are whispering be?

AT HARVEST-TIME

The trees stand waiting;
The windmills are prating
And gesticulating—
But what is debating?
What do they wait to hear or to see?

We shall soon know, I trust—
Whew, the wind! just
A soft, rapid gust,
That swirls about the dust
In the serpentine green lane, and the straws upon
       the lea!

The light white mill divines;
I can see him making signs
To his heavy black brother;
They nod to each other—
"Hail-fellows-well-met with the Wind are we!"

And my lady in her bower,
Or her parlour, or her tower,
Says, "In about an hour
We shall have a thunder-shower '——
Shine or storm, pretty lady, keep a kiss for me!

SEE-SAW

I SAID to the babe, out of swaddling bands,
  As it kicked up its heels, and flung out its
      hands,
And blew little bubbles, and cried, and crew,
" You innocent dear! But I wouldn't be you!"

" And yet I don't know : you have never to think;
You have only to snuggle, and sleep, and drink,
And, in spite of original sin, grow fat.
Yes, really, one might do worse than that!"

I said to the schoolboy, "You joyous elf!"—
I mean, I murmured the thing to myself,
Or he would have laughed—"Get out, sir, do!
I have half a mind to wish I were you!"

99

SEE-SAW

He looked so jolly, that scaramouch did,
As gay as a Clown, as bold as the Cid;
But then I remembered task and taws—
There is always something to make one pause.

And my dot of a daughter, she says, " Papa!
I wish you would make me my own mamma!
She *is* so happy, she *is* so nice!
And then I would give you my three white
    mice!"

Says I, "You're a duck, a dear, a pearl!"
But really my brain was inclined to whirl;
"There is always something," I thought; "but
    why?
Perhaps we shall know of it by-and-bye."

So I went to my bed, and I dreamed that night
Of a saint in heaven, all shining white.
"Sweet, fair-eyed seraph!" said I, in sleep;
"I wish I were you, in the rest you keep!"

And yet at the word I thought, in bed,
Of wife, and Walter, and Winifred ;
The Christmas bells my slumber broke:
"There is always something!" thought I, and
    woke.

GREAT, WIDE, BEAUTIFUL, WONDER-
FUL WORLD

GREAT, wide, beautiful, wonderful World,
    With the wonderful water round you
  curled,
And the wonderful grass upon your breast—
World, you are beautifully drest.

The wonderful air is over me,
And the wonderful wind is shaking the tree,
It walks on the water, and whirls the mills,
And talks to itself on the tops of the hills.

You friendly Earth! how far do you go,
With the wheat-fields that nod and the rivers
   that flow,
With cities and gardens, and cliffs, and isles,
And people upon you for thousands of miles?

Ah, you are so great, and I am so small,
I tremble to think of you, World, at all;
And yet, when I said my prayers to-day,
A whisper inside me seemed to say,
" You are more than the Earth, though you are
   such a dot:
You can love and think, and the Earth cannot!"

KITTENS AND CHICKENS

THAT is the Kitten,
The one in black
That you see at the back,
Whose heart was smitten
(For kittens have hearts
As well as brains
And other parts,
For pleasures and pains)—
Was smitten, I say,
On a sunshiny day,
By a callow chicken,
And made a picking
Of the chicken's bones
Out there, on the stones,
To the great disgust
Of the mother Hen,
Who came up then,

When the feast was ended,
And the undefended
Fowl just swallowed!
And the Hen was followed
By the Cock well-grown,
Who seemed disgusted
That the Hen had trusted
The chicken alone.

It was on the next day
That the Cat did essay
To visit the place
Of this disgrace,
In search of a chicken
Again for picking;
But now the Cock,
As firm as a rock,
Beholding the Kitten,
With rage was smitten,
And stuck out his chest,
And set up his crest,
And crowed defiance,
Like an army of lions,
To the Kitten who there,
With his tail in the air,
Saw that the hens,—
Three in number,—
Were not in slumber,
And so had the sense

KITTENS AND CHICKENS

To take his departure,
Like the arrow of an archer
Swift from a bow,
And left the Cock,
As firm as a rock,
To ruffle and crow,
All under the door,
As we said before,
With nothing to tire him,
And the hens to admire him.

In a corner was sitting
Another Kitten,
White, not black,
Who heard the clack,
And knowing the story
Of the chicken gory,
And, seeing the Cock
Defying the other
(It was her brother!)
Had trepidations
And meditations
About taking chickens,
And such, for pickings.
But cats will be cats
The whole world long!

THE MAKING OF THE MUSIC

"MAKE us a song, then, mother dear!
       Sweet to think of, and sweet to sing,"
Said the little daughter and the little son;
    Their lips were gay, and their eyes were clear—
      "And let the song be an easy one,
          Sweet to think of, and sweet to sing."

"Sweet to think of, and sweet to hear?
How shall I make it, children dear?
The night is falling, the winds are rough;
What will you give me to make it of?"

"No, mother dear, the winds are soft,
And the sky is blue and clear aloft,
And oh! we can give you things enough
To make the beautiful music of.

106

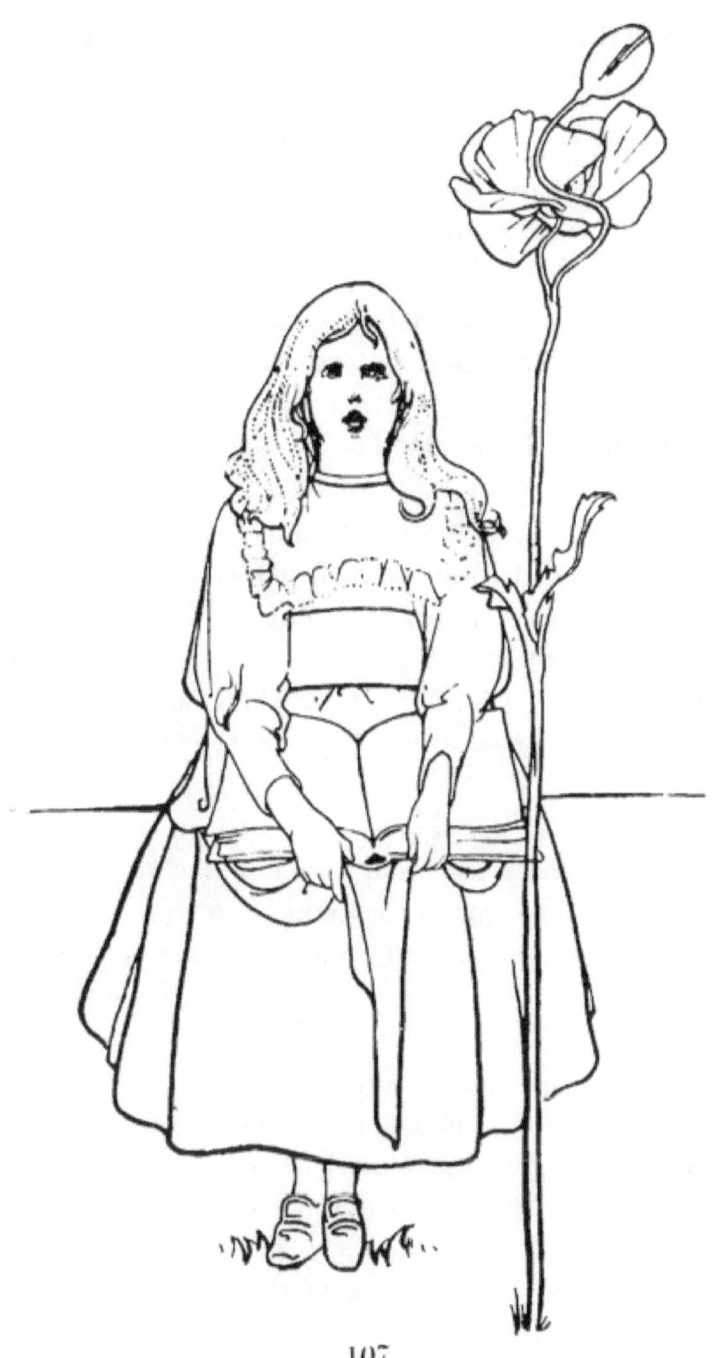

THE MAKING OF THE MUSIC

"We will give you the morning and afternoon,
We will give you the sun, and a white full moon;
You shall have all our prettiest toys,
And fields and flowers, and girls and boys.

"We will give you a bird, and a ship at sea,
And a golden cloud, and an almond-tree,
A picture gay, a river that runs,
A chime of bells, and hot cross-buns.

"You may have roses and rubies rare,
And silks and satins beyond compare,
A sceptre and crown, a queen, a king,
And beautiful dreams, and everything!
We will give you all that we think or know—
The song will be sweet if you make it so."

Then the mother smiled as she began
To make the music, and sweet it ran,
And easy enough, for a strain or two;
And the children said, "Mother, the song will
    do!"

But soon the melody ran less clear;
There came a pause, and a wandering tear,
And a thought that went back many a year;
And the children fancied the music long,
And asked, "What have you put into the song
That we did not tell you, mother dear?"

THE RACE OF THE FLOWERS

THE trees and the flowers seem running a
    race,
  But none treads down the other;
And neither thinks it his disgrace
  To be later than his brother.

Yet the pear-tree shouts to the lilac-tree,
  " Make haste, for the Spring is late ! "
And the lilac whispers to the chestnut-tree
  (Because he is so great),
" Pray you, great sir, be quick, be quick,
For down below we are blossoming thick ! "

Then the chestnut hears, and comes out in bloom,
  White, or pink, to the tip-top boughs—
Oh, why not grow higher, there's plenty of room,
  You beautiful tree, with the sky for your
    house ?
Then like music they seem to burst out together,
  The little and the big, with a beautiful burst ;
They sweeten the wind, they paint the weather,
  And no one remembers which was first :
    White rose, red rose,
    Bud rose, shed rose,
    Larkspur, and lily, and the rest,
    North, south, east, west,
    June, July, August, September !

Ever so late in the year will come
Many a red geranium,
  And chrysanthemums up to November !
Then the winter has overtaken them all,
The fogs and the rains begin to fall,

THE RACE OF THE FLOWERS

And the flowers, after running their races,
Are weary, and shut up their little faces,
And under the ground they go to sleep.
Is it very far down? Yes, ever so deep.

POLLY

BROWN eyes,
   Straight nose ;
Dirt pies,
   Rumpled clothes ;

Torn books,
   Spoilt toys ;
Arch looks,
   Unlike a boy's ;

Little rages,
   Obvious arts ;
(Three her age is,)
   Cakes, tarts ;

Falling down
   Off chairs ;
Breaking crown
   Down stairs ;

POLLY

Catching flies
  On the pane;
Deep sighs,—
  Cause not plain;

Bribing you
  With kisses
For a few
  Farthing blisses;

Wide awake,
  As you hear,
"Mercy's sake,
  Quiet, dear!"

New shoes,
  New frock;
Vague views
  Of what's o'clock

When it's time
  To go to bed,
And scorn sublime
  Of what is said;

Folded hands,
  Saying prayers,
Understands
  Not, nor cares;

POLLY

Thinks it odd,
　　Smiles away;
Yet may God
　　Hear her pray!

Bedgown white,
　　Kiss Dolly;
Good-night!—
　　That's Polly,

Fast asleep,
　　As you see;
Heaven keep
　　My girl for me!

THE WINDMILL

NOW, who will live in the windmill, who,
    With the powdery miller-man?
The miller is one, but who'll make two,
    To share his loaf and can?

"O, I will live with the miller, I!
  To grind the corn is grand ;
The great black sails go up on high,
  And come down to the land!"

Now who will be the miller's bride?
  The miller's in haste to wed
A girl in her pride, with a sash at her side,
  A girl with a curly head!

"O, I will be the miller's wife ;
  The dust is all my joy ;
To live in a windmill all my life
  Would be a sweet employ!"

Then spake the goblin of the sails
  (You heard, but could not see),
"The wickedest man of the hills and dales,
  The miller-man is he!

"None ever dwelt in the mill before
  But died by the miller's steel ;
The whiskered rats lap up their gore,
  He grinds their bones to meal!"

O gossiping goblin, my dreams will be bad,
  You tell such dreadful tales!
O mill, how secret you seem! how mad,
  How wicked you look, black sails!

THE GIRL THAT GARIBALDI KISSED

OH, where's the little maid
    That Garibaldi kissed?
She ought to be displayed,
    She shall be, I insist,

Command, resolve, determine,—
    Beneath a tent of gold,
In swan's-down and in ermine,
    If Christmas should be cold!

THE GIRL THAT GARIBALDI KISSED

I am not very rich,
  But would give a golden guinea
To see that little witch,
  That happy pick-a-ninny !

He bowed to my own daughter,
  And Polly is her name ;
She wore a shirt of slaughter,
  Of Garibaldi flame,—

Of course I mean of scarlet ;
  But the girl he kissed—who knows ?—
May be named Selina Charlotte,
  And dressed in yellow clothes !

I look for her in church,
  I seek her in the crowd ;
Some bellman on a perch
  Ought to ask for her out loud !

I would offer a reward,
  But I might get cheated then,
And I cannot well afford
  To make that guinea ten.

She may live up in Lancashire,
  All in her yellow gown,
Or down in Hankypankyshire,
  Or here in London town.

THE GIRL THAT GARIBALDI KISSED

She may be on board a steamer
  Upon the briny sea—
O stewardess ! esteem her,
  For a glorious girl is she !

Perhaps at some academy
  Her *Télémaque* is read—
They would think it very bad of me
  To turn her little head !

She may be doing fancy-work,
  She may be taking tea ;
But I wish some necromancy-work
  Would bring that girl to me !

For I would dress the little girl
  That Garibaldi kissed
In a necklace all of precious pearl,
  With a bracelet for her wrist,

With diamonds in her stomacher,
  And garlands in her hair ;
She should sit, for folks to come at her,
  All in a silver chair ;

And no one would be rude
  To Garibaldi's pet,—
The sight would do the people good,
  They never would forget !

THE GIRL THAT GARIBALDI KISSED

Oh glorious is the girl
   Whom such a man has kissed,
The proudest duke or earl
   Stands lower in the list!

It would be a happy plan
   For everything that's human,
If the pet of such a man
   Should grow to such a woman!

If she does as much in her way
   As he has done in his,—
Turns bad things topsy-turvey,
   And sad things into bliss,—
Oh, we shall not need a survey
   To find that little miss,
Grown to a woman worthy
   Of Garibaldi's kiss!

SEEING GOD

IT is dark, the night is come,
    And the world is hushed and dumb;
Sleep, my darling; God is here!—
Shall I see Him, mother dear?

It is day, the sun is bright,
And the world is laid in light;
Wake, my darling, God is here!—
Shall I see Him, mother dear?

SEEING GOD

Not the day's awakening light,
Babe, can show thee God aright;
Not the dark, that brings thee sleep,
Him can from my darling keep.

Day and night are His, to fill:
We are His, to do His will;
Do His will, and, never fear,
Thou shalt see Him, baby dear.

FAIR LADY, RARE LADY

FAIR lady, rare lady,
  Light on the lea
Wandering, and pondering—
  "Oh, bring him to me!"

124

FAIR LADY, RARE LADY

Gallant knight, valiant knight,
  Swift on the sea
Sailing, prevailing,
  Thy shallop shall be!

Ringing bells, singing bells,
  Chime merrilie!
Brave knight and lady bright
  Wedded shall be!

THE ABSENT BOY

I KNOW an absent-minded boy,
To meditate is all his joy;
He seldom does the thing he ought
Because he is so rapt in thought.

At marbles he can never win;
He wears his waistcoat outside in;
He cannot add a sum up right;
And often he is not polite.

THE ABSENT BOY

His mother cries, "My poor heart breaks,
Because the child makes such mistakes;
He never knows," she says with sighs,
"Which side his bread the butter lies!"

One day, absorbed in meditation,
He roamed into a railway station,
And in a corner of a train
Sat down, with inattentive brain.

They rang the bell, the whistle blew,
They shook the flags, the engine flew;
But all the noise did not induce
This boy to quit his mood abstruse.

And when three hours were past and gone
He found himself at Something*ton;*
"What is this place?" he sighed in vain,
For railway men can not speak plain.

When he got home his parents had
To pay his fare, which was too bad;
More than two hundred miles, alas!
The Absent Boy had gone first-class.

For fear he should, in absentness,
Forget his own name and address
Whilst he pursues his meditations,
And so be lost to his relations,

THE ABSENT BOY

Would it be best that he should wear
A collar like our Tray? or bear
His name and home in indigo
Pricked on his shoulder, or below?

The chief objection to this plan
Is, that his father is a man
Who often moves. If we begin
To prick the Boy's home on his skin,

Before long he will be tattooed
With indigo from head to foot:
Perhaps a label on his chest
Would meet the difficulty best.

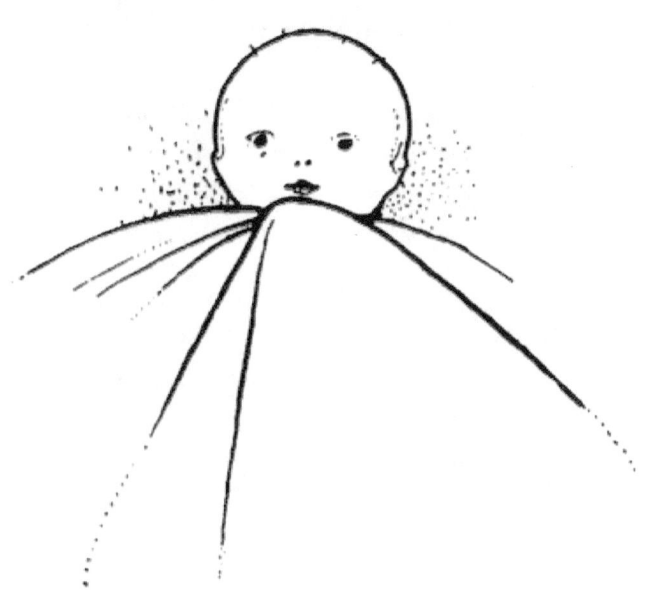

MORNING

WELCOME to the new To-day!
   Yesterday is past and gone;
Good-bye Night and Twilight gray,
  Earth has put the Morning on:

Morning on the high hill's shoulder,
  On the valley's lap so soft,
On the river running colder,
  On the trees with heads aloft.

MORNING

All night Baby thought of nothing,
　Sleep took care of Baby dear;
Baby, too, has fine new clothing,
　Now the sweet To-day is here.

Tell me, without many guesses,—
　Come! it is not much to con,—
Tell me what my Babe's new dress is?
　Babe has put the Morning on!

THE RISING, WATCHING MOON

AH, the moon is watching me!
 Red, and round as round can be,
Over the house and the top of the tree
Rising slowly. We shall see
Something happen very soon ;—
Hide me from the dreadful moon!

THE RISING, WATCHING MOON

Slowly, surely, rising higher,
Soon she will be as high as the spire!
It seems as if something must happen then
To all the world, and all the men!
Oh, I dare not think, for I am not wise—
I must look away, I must shut my eyes!

THE FLOWERS

WHEN Love arose in heart and deed,
　　To wake the world to greater joy,
"What can she give me now?" said Greed,
　　Who thought to win some costly toy.

He rose, he ran, he stooped, he clutched,
　　And soon the flowers, that Love let fall,
In Greed's hot grasp were frayed and smutched,
　　And Greed said, "Flowers! can this be all?"

THE FLOWERS

He flung them down, and went his way,
   He cared no jot for thyme or rose;
But boys and girls came out to play,
   And some took these, and some took those,

Red, blue, and white, and green and gold;
   And at their touch the dew returned,
And all the bloom a thousand fold,
   So red, so ripe, the roses burned.

THE PENANCE OF THE LITTLE MAID

I MET a fair maiden, I saw her plain,
  In the five-acre when the corn was mellow,
Counting her fingers again and again,
  Her kirtle was green, her hair was yellow.

THE PENANCE OF THE LITTLE MAID

"Oh, what are you counting, fair maid?" said I,
   "Counting, I will be bound, your treasures?"
"Oh no, kind sir," she made sad reply,
   "Counting, for penance, my unshared pleasures."

Her head was bent low, and slowly went she;
If she goes on straight, she must come to the
    sea!

Blow, blow, south wind, the year's on the turn;
Creep, little blue-bell, close under the fern!

I hope that the penance the little maid is doing
Will be finished before winter comes with rattle,
    rain, and ruin?

"Oh yes, kind sir, my penance will be over"
   (She told me in a dream last night, I know it
    will come true),
"Come and look for me next summer, when the
    bee is in the clover,
And I will share my pleasures then with you,
    you, you!"

FRODGEDOBBULUM'S FANCY

I

D ID you ever see Giant Frodgedobbulum,
    With his double great-toe and his double
        great thumb?

137

FRODGEDOBBULUM'S FANCY

Did you ever hear Giant Frodgedobbulum,
Saying *Fa-fe-fi* and *fo-far-fum*?

He shakes the earth as he walks along,
As deep as the sea, as far as Hong-kong!

He is a giant and no mistake;
With teeth like the prongs of a garden rake!

II

The Giant Frodgedobbulum got out of bed,
Sighing, "Heigh-ho! that I were but wed!"

The Giant Frodgedobbulum sat in his chair,
Saying, "Why should a giant be wanting a fair?"

The Giant Frodgedobbulum said to his boots,
"The first maid I meet I will wed, if she suits!"

They were Magic Boots, and they laughed as he
  spoke—
"Oh, ho," says the giant, "you think it's a
  joke?"

III

So he put on his boots, and came stumping
   down,
Clatter and clump, into Banbury town—

He did not fly into Banbury,
For plenty of time to walk had he!

He kicked at the gate—" Within there, ho!"
" Oh, what is your name?" says the porter Slow.

" Oh, the Giant Frodgedobblum am I,
For a wife out of Banbury town I sigh!"

Up spake the porter, bold and free,
" Your room we prefer to your company."

Up spake Frodgedobbulum, free and bold,
" I will build up your town with silver and
   gold!"

Up spake Marjorie, soft and small,
  I will not be your wife at all!"

The giant knocked in the gate with his feet,
And there stood Marjorie in the street!

FRODGEDOBBULUM'S FANCY

She was nine years old, she was lissome and fair,
And she wore emeralds in her hair.

She could dance like a leaf, she could sing like a
thrush,
She was bold as the north wind, and sweet as a
blush.

Her father tanned, her mother span,
"But Marjorie shall marry a gentleman,—

Silks and satins, I'll lay you a crown!"—
So said the people in Banbury town.

Such was Marjorie—and who should come
To woo her but this Frodgedobbulum,

A vulgar giant, who wore no gloves,
And very pig-headed in his loves!

IV

They rang the alarum, and in the steeple
They tolled the church-bells to rouse the people.

But all the people in Banbury town
Could not put Frodgedobbulum down.

The tanner thought to stab him dead—
"Somebody pricked me?" the giant said.

The mother wept—"I do not care,"
Said F.—"Why should I be wanting a fair?"

He snatched up Marjorie, stroked his boot,
And fled; with Banbury in pursuit!

"What ho, my boots! put forth your power!
Carry me sixty miles an hour!"

In ditches and dykes, over stocks and stones,
The Banbury people fell, with groans.

Frodgedobbulum passed over river and tree,
Gallopy-gallop, with Marjorie;—

The people beneath her Marjorie sees
Of the size of mites in an Oxford cheese!

V

Castle Frodgedobbulum sulked between
Two bleak hills, in a deep ravine.

It was always dark there, and always drear,
The same time of day and the same time of year.

FRODGEDOBBULUM'S FANCY

The walls of the castle were slimy and black,
There were dragons in front, and toads at the
    back.

Spiders there were, and of vampires lots;
Ravens croaked round the chimney-pots.

Seven bull-dogs barked in the hall;
Seven wild cats did caterwaul!

The giant said, with a smirk on his face,
"My Marjorie, this is a pretty place;

As Mrs. F. you will lead, with me,
A happier life than in Banbury!

Pour out my wine, and comb my hair,
And put me to sleep in my easy chair;

But, first, my boots I will kick away"—
And Marjorie answered, "*S'il vous plait!*"

Then the giant mused, "It befits my station
To marry a lady of education;

But who would have thought this Banbury wench
Was so accomplished, and could speak French?"

FRODGEDOBBULUM'S FANCY

Did you ever hear Frodgedobbulum snore?
He shook the castle from roof to floor!

Fast asleep as a pig was he—
" And very much like one!" thought Marjorie.

VI

Then Marjorie stood on a leathern chair,
And opened the window to the air.

The bats flap, the owls hoot—
Majorie lifted the giant's boot!

The ravens shriek, the owls hoot—
Majorie got into the giant's boot!

And Marjorie said, " I can reach the moon
Before you waken, you big buffoon!"

Once, twice, three times, and away,—
" Which is the road to Banbury, pray?"

The Boot made answer, " Hah, hah! hoh, hoh!
The road to Banbury town I know."

VII

The giant awoke in his easy chair,
Saying, " Ho, little Marjorie, are you there ?

A stoup of wine, to be spiced the same !—
Exquisite Marjorie, *je vous aime !* "

Now where was Marjorie ? Safe and sound
In the Magic Boot she cleared the ground.

Frodgedobbulum groaned—" I am bereft !
The left boot's gone, and the right is left !—

The window's open ! I'll bet a crown
The chit is off to Banbury town !

But follow, follow, my faithful Boot !
One is enough for the pursuit ;

And back to my arms the wench shall come
As sure as my name's Frodgedobbulum ! "

VIII

Hasty Frodgedobbulum, being a fool,
Forgot of the Magic Boots the rule.

FRODGEDOBBULUM'S FANCY

They were made on a right and a left boot-tree,
But he put the wrong leg in the boot, you see!

It was a terrible mistake
For even a giant in love to make—

Terrible in its consequences,
Frightful to any man's seven senses!

Down came a thunderbolt, rumble and glare!
Frodgedobbulum Castle blew up in the air!

The giant, deprived of self-control,
Was carried away to the very North Pole;

For such was the magic rule. Poor F.
Now sits on the peak of the Arctic cliff!

The point is so sharp it makes him shrink;
The northern streamers, they make him blink;

One boot on, and one boot off,
He shivers and shakes, and thinks, with a cough,

"Safe in Banbury Marjorie dwells;
Marjorie will marry some one else!"

IX

And so Frodgedobbulum, the giant,
Sits on the North Pole incompliant.

He blinks at the snow with its weary white;
He blinks at the spears of the northern light;

Kicks out with one boot; says, "Fi-fo-fum!
I am the Giant Frodgedobbulum!"

But who cares whether he is or not,
Living in such an inclement spot?

Banbury town is the place for me,
And a kiss from merry Marjorie,

With the clerk in the vestry to see all fair—
For she wears orange-flowers in her hair!

She can dance like a leaf, she can sing like a
    thrush,
She is bold as the north wind, and sweet as a
    blush;

Her father he tans, her mother she spins;
Frodgedobbulum sits on the Pole for his sins;

FRODGEDOBBULUM'S FANCY

But here comes Marjorie, white as milk,
A rose on her bosom as soft as silk,

On her finger a gay gold ring;
The bridegroom holds up his head like a king!

Marjorie has married a gentleman;
Who knows when the wedding began?

THE GUINEA-PIG

"OH, I never would be a guinea-pig, never!
    They have so little brains!"—
The guinea-pig sprang, and—wasn't it clever?—
    He hid in the raspberry canes.

They scratched their fingers, they taxed their
        wits,
    To get the guinea-pig out;
They nearly laughed themselves to fits
    To see him run about.

THE GUINEA-PIG

The old and the young, the patient, the bold,
  Were in that companie;
But the guinea-pig baffled the young and the old,
  And merrily scampered he.

You thought you had him, but oh, mistake!
  You grappled a lump of mould—
The guinea-pig stuck to the raspberry brake
  As hath before been told.

"Oh, make me into a guinea-pig, make,
  And never mind what I said;
For then I can hide in the raspberry brake,
  When it's time to go to bed."

LITTLE BOY BLUE

ALL in the morning early,
   The Little Boy in Blue
(The grass with rain is pearly)
   Has thought of something new.

He saddled dear old Dobbin;
   He had but half-a-crown;
And jogging, cantering, bobbing,
   He came to London town.

LITTLE BOY BLUE

The sheep were in the meadows,
  The cows were in the corn;
Beneath the city shadows
  At last he stood forlorn.

He stood beneath Bow steeple,
  That is in London town;
And tried to count the people
  As they went up and down.

Oh, there was not a daisy,
  And not a buttercup;
The air was thick and hazy,
  The Blue Boy gave it up.

The houses, next, in London,
  He thought that he would count;
But still the sum was undone,
  So great was the amount.

He could not think of robbing,
  He had but half-a-crown;
And so he mounted Dobbin,
  And rode back from the town.

The sheep were in the meadows,
  The cows were in the corn;
Amid the evening shadows
  He stood where he was born.

MISS HOOPER

MISS HOOPER was a little girl,
    Whose head was always in a whirl;
For she had hoop upon the head—
"My precious, precious hoop!" she said.

MISS HOOPER

Trundling a hoop was her delight
From breakfast time to nearly night,
She loved it so! and, truth to tell,
At last she drove her hoop too well.

That hoop began to go one day
As if it never meant to stay;
Of course the girl would not give in,
But followed it through thick and thin.

The King and Queen came out to see
What sort of hoop this hoop might be;
My Lady said, "I think, my Lord,
That hoop goes of its own accord."

This vexed the little girl, and so
She gave the hoop another blow,
And off it went—oh, just like mad—
She ran with all the strength she had.

Her hat-strings slipped, her hat hung back,
And soon she felt her waistband crack,
Her dear long hair flew out behind her,—
Her parents sent forth scouts to find her.

The King leapt on his swiftest horse,
And followed her with all his force;
Her father cried, " A thousand pound
To get my girl back safe and sound!"

MISS HOOPER

Some people came and made a dash
To pull her backward by the sash,
But all in vain—she did not stop—
At last she fainted, with a flop.

When she came to she sighed, with pain,
"I'll never touch a hoop again!"
Is it not sad, when girls and boys
Go to excess like this with toys?

As for the hoop, the people say
It kept on going night and day,
Turning the corners, quite correct,—
A thing which you would not expect.

MISS HOOPER

And so it lived, a hoop at large,
Which no one dared to take in charge;
Of course it thinned, but kept its shape,
A sort of hoop of wooden tape.

It thinned till people took a glass
To see the ghostly circle pass,
And only stopped—the facts are so—
When there was nothing left to go.

A SHOOTING SONG

TO shoot, to shoot, would be my delight,
   To shoot the cats that howl in the night;
To shoot the lion, the wolf, the bear,
To shoot the mad dogs out in the square.

I learnt to shoot with a pop-gun good,
Made out of a branch of elder-wood;
It was round, and long, full half a yard,
The plug was strong, the pellets were hard.

A SHOOTING SONG

I should like to shoot with a bow of yew,
As the English at Agincourt used to do;
The strings of a thousand bows went twang!
And a thousand arrows whizzed and sang!

On Hounslow Heath I should like to ride,
With a great horse-pistol at my side:
It is dark—hark! A robber, I know!
Click! crick-crack! and away we go!

I will shoot with a double-barrelled gun,
Two bullets are better than only one;
I will shoot some rooks to put in a pie;
I will shoot an eagle up in the sky.

I once shot a bandit in a dream,
In a mountain-pass I heard a scream;
I rescued the lady and set her free,
" Do not fear, madam, lean on me!"

With a boomerang I could not aim;
A poison blow-pipe would be the same;
A double-barrelled is my desire,
Get out of the way—one, two, three, fire!

A FISHING SONG

THERE was a boy whose name was Phinn,
  And he was fond of fishing;
His father could not keep him in,
  Nor all his mother's wishing.

A FISHING SONG

His life's ambition was to land
　A fish of several pound weight;
The chief thing he could understand
　Was hooks, or worms for ground-bait.

The worms crept out, the worms crept in,
　From every crack and pocket;
He had a worm-box made of tin,
　With proper worms to stock it.

He gave his mind to breeding worms
　As much as he was able;
His sister spoke in angry terms
　To see them on the table.

You found one walking up the stairs,
　You found one in a bonnet,
Or, in the bed-room, unawares,
　You set your foot upon it.

A FISHING SONG

Worms, worms, worms for bait!
  Roach, and dace, and gudgeon!
With rod and line to Twickenham Ait
  To-morrow he is trudging!

O worms and fishes day and night!
  Such was his sole ambition;
I'm glad to think you are not quite
  So very fond of fishing!

SHOCKHEADED CICELY AND THE TWO BEARS

"O YES! O yes! O yes! ding dong!"
     The bellman's voice is loud and strong;
So is his bell: "O yes! ding dong!"

SHOCKHEADED CICELY

He wears a red coat with golden lace;
See how the people of the place
Come running to hear what the bellman says!

"O yes! Sir Nicholas Hildebrand
Has just returned from the Holy Land,
And freely offers his heart and hand—

O yes! O yes! O yes! ding dong!"—
All the women hurry along,
Maids and widows, a chattering throng.

"O sir, you are hard to understand!
To whom does he offer his heart and hand?
Explain your meaning, we do command!"

"O yes! ding dong! you shall understand!
O yes! Sir Nicholas Hildebrand
Invites the ladies of this land

To feast with him in his castle strong
This very day at three. Ding dong!
O yes! O yes! O yes! ding dong!"

Then all the women went off to dress,
Mary, Margaret, Bridget, Bess,
Patty, and more than I can guess.

SHOCKHEADED CICELY

They powdered their hair with golden dust,
And bought new ribbons—they said they must—
But none of them painted, we will trust.

Long before the time arrives,
All the women that could be wives
Are dressed within an inch of their lives.

Meanwhile, Sir Nicholas Hildebrand
Had brought with him from the Holy Land
A couple of bears—oh, that was grand!

He tamed the bears, and they loved him true,
Whatever he told them they would do—
Hark! 'tis the town clock striking two!

II

Among the maidens of low degree
The poorest of all was Cicely—
A shabbier girl could hardly be.

"O I should like to see the feast,
But my frock is old, my shoes are pieced,
My hair is rough!"—(it never was greased).

SHOCKHEADED CICELY

The clock struck three! She durst not go!
But she heard the band, and to see the show
Crept after the people that went in a row.

When Cicely came to the castle gate
The porter exclaimed, " Miss Shaggypate,
The hall is full, and you come too late!"

Just then the music made a din,
Flute, and cymbal, and culverin,
And Cicely, with a squeeze, got in!

Oh what a sight! full fifty score
Of dames that Cicely knew, and more,
Filling the hall from daïs to door!

The dresses were like a garden-bed,
Green and gold, and blue and red,—
Poor Cicely thought of her tossy head!

She heard the singing—she heard the clatter—
Clang of flagon, and clink of platter—
But, oh, the feast was no such matter!

For she saw Sir Nicholas himself,
Raised on a daïs just like a shelf,
And fell in love with him—shabby elf!

Her heart beat quick ; aside she stept,
Under the tapestry she crept,
Touzling her tossy hair, and wept !

Her cheeks were wet, her eyes were red—
" Who makes that noise ? " the ladies said ;
" Turn out that girl with the shaggy head ! "

III

Just then there was heard a double roar,
That shook the place, both wall and floor :
Everybody looked to the door.

It was a roar, it was a growl ;
The ladies set up a little howl,
And flapped and clucked like frightened fowl.

Sir Hildebrand for silence begs—
In walk the bears on their hinder legs,
Wise as owls, and merry as grigs !

The dark girls tore their hair of sable ;
The fair girls hid underneath the table ;
Some fainted ; to move they were not able

But most of them could scream and screech—
Sir Nicholas Hildebrand made a speech—
"Order! ladies, I do beseech!"

The bears looked hard at Cicely
Because her hair hung wild and free—
"Related to us, miss, you must be!"

Then Cicely, filling two plates of gold
As full of cherries as they could hold,
Walked up to the bears, and spoke out bold:—

"Welcome to you! and to *you*, Mr. Bear!
Will you take a chair? will *you* take a chair?"
"This is an honour, we do declare!"

Sir Hildebrand strode up to see,
Saying, "Who may this maiden be?
Ladies, this is the wife for me!"

Almost before they could understand,
He took up Cicely by the hand,
And danced with her a saraband.

Her hair was as rough as a parlour broom,
It swung, it swirled all round the room—
Those ladies were vexed, we may presume.

SHOCKHEADED CICELY

Sir Nicholas kissed her on the face,
And set her beside him on the daïs,
And made her the lady of the place.

The nuptials soon they did prepare,
With a silver comb for Cicely's hair:
There were bands of music everywhere.

And in that beautiful bridal show
Both the bears were seen to go
Upon their hind legs to and fro!

Now every year on the wedding-day
The boys and girls come out to play,
And scramble for cherries as they may,

With a cheer for this and the other bear,
And a cheer for Sir Nicholas, free and fair,
And a cheer for Cis of the tossy hair—

With one cheer more (if you will wait)
For every girl with a curly pate
Who keeps her hair in a proper state.

Sing bear's grease! curling-irons to sell!
Sing combs and brushes! sing tortoise-shell!
O yes! ding dong! the crier, the bell!
—Isn't this a pretty tale to tell?

MOTHER'S JOY

BABY boy was Mother's joy,
And Mother nursed him sweetly;
Baby's skin was pink and thin,
And mother dressed him neatly.

MOTHER'S JOY

Baby boy was Mother's joy,
  But sometimes cried a-plenty;
Mother mild said, "Oh, my child!"
  And gave him kisses twenty.

Baby boy was Mother's joy,
  Wide awake or sleeping;
Mother said, "God overhead
  Have thee in His keeping!"

THE BABY

WHO can tell what Baby thinks?

I can, I!

Who knows what she means when she crows or blinks?

I do, I!

THE BABY

She thinks that a picture is good to eat,
>> *She does, she !*
She thinks she should love to swallow her feet.
>> *Hah, hah, he !*

She thinks when I touch the piano-keys,
>> *La, si, do !*
That *I* make the noise, as I do when I sneeze.
>> *Hah, hah, hoh !*

When I put her fat hand on the key-board shelf,
>> *Do, re, mi !*
She fancies she makes the noise herself.
>> *She, sir, she !*

She thinks she could swallow the lamp entire.
>> *Flame, flame, flame !*
She thinks she should like to cuddle the fire.
>> *(Same, same, same !)*

I wished her a pair of leather shoes—
>> *I did, did !*
Nothing like leather—and riper views.
>> *Kid, kid, kid !*

But whether the wit or the leather comes first,
>> *(Post, hoc, hoc !)*
One thing I know—she *will* be nursed.
>> *Rock, rock, rock !*

171

THE BABY

And Baby's mamma is a beautiful nurse,
> *Joy, joy, joy!*

She might go farther and fare much worse,
> *With a boy, boy, boy!*

For though I have studied her wits and ways,
> *Bye-bye-bye!*

I couldn't take charge of her, nights and days.
> *Cry, cry, cry!*

WHAT WILL AUNTIE SEND?

OH, do you know Aunt Mary Ann,
    The dearest Aunt since time began,
Aunt Kate, Aunt Jane, Aunt Edith Ellen,
Aunt—oh, but never mind the spelling!

WHAT WILL AUNTIE SEND?

She lives up North, she lives down South,
Sweet are the kisses of her mouth;
She lives out East, she lives out West,
Bona puella Auntie est!

Always about the time of year
When Christmas Day is drawing near,
Auntie goes in for treats and toys,
And things, you know, for girls and boys.

Then, with a smile upon her lips,
She sits and thinks of tops and tips,
And takes her pen and writes to us,
My sister Fan, and me—that's 'Gus.

She walks Cheapside, she walks the Strand,
And Paul's Churchyard, with purse in hand,
She looks at dolls, she looks at drums,
And boxes full of bloomy plums.

She goes and finds out picture books,
And jewellery hung on hooks;
She knows the games we like to play;
She buys things, all to give away!

The loveliest things in every part
She goes and gets them all by heart,
And then sits down, with time to think,
And writes to us with pen and ink.

WHAT WILL AUNTIE SEND?

I know her thoughts,—she thinks of us,—
She thinks, "What would be nice for 'Gus?'
She dips in Santa Klaus's pouch:
"What shall I send that scaramouch?"

She keeps it dark, but writes to say
She will be here for Christmas Day;
And when I know that Aunt will come,
Quam felix puer ego sum!

LORDS-AND-LADIES

L ORDS-AND-LADIES, red and white,
    By the river growing,
Red-and-white is my delight,
    When the stream is flowing.

I will be a lord to-day
    (Round the world is going),
Will you be a lady gay?
    (Roses, roses blowing).
176

LORDS-AND-LADIES

"I will be your lady fair,
  If you will show duty :"
I will love beyond compare,
  You shall be my beauty.

Lords-and-ladies, red and white,
  By the river growing ;
Red-and-white is my delight,
  When the stream is flowing.

THE DOG AND THE PATCH OF
MOONSHINE

A HARVEST moon! Was ever seen
A harvest moon so bright?
The crowded ivy, darkly green,
Was touched with primrose white.

The quiet skies uncovered lay,
And, far as you could see,
The night was like a ghostly day
On road, and field, and tree.

Silence and light! Will nothing speak
  In the light and silence wide?
O lady moon, your other cheek
  Why do you always hide?

Sweet on the air was the jessamine,
  As I stood at my gate;
Yet I shuddered, and thought, "I will go in,—
  The silence is too great!"

I looked to where the hill-tops showed
  Behind the poplars green,
When there came trotting down the road
  A dog—the dog was lean;

And you could tell, as he came by,
  He had no friend on earth,
Nobody in whose partial eye
  He was of any worth.

His tail hung down; his matted hair
  Was like a worn-out thatch;
This dog came trotting up to where
  The moonlight made a patch,

Falling between two poplar-trees;
  And there the dog turned round,
Round, and round, by slow degrees—
  Then crouched upon the ground.

THE DOG AND PATCH OF MOONSHINE

And I brought forth some broken food,
   And cried, "Old dog, get up!
That patch of moonlight may be good,
   But on it you cannot sup."

He came away—came many a pace,
   And took what I bestowed;
Then, being refreshed, snuffed all the place,
   And up and down the road.

I showed him where the thick grass grew
   Against a sheltering wall;
I said, "Here is a bed for you,
   With half-a-house and all."

But two hours after—I kept watch
   From my bedroom window-pane—
I saw that on that moony patch
   He had lain down again!

And in the morning he was gone.—
   What charm was it he found
In sleeping where the moonlight shone
   In a patch upon the ground?
He might have slept where he had his bone,
   Where the moon shone all around!

THE DOG AND PATCH OF MOONSHINE

I am a superstitious man,
   And it is my delight
To think there was a magic plan,
   A meaning, in that night!

That magic dog that lay i' the moon,
   He will come back to me,
A fairy princess bright and boon,
   Whom I that night set free!

There was a mystery in the air,
   And in the primrose light;
The silence seemed to say, " Prepare!
   It shall be done to-night!"

And could that mystery only mean
   A dog that was not fat?
I saw a glint of elfin green
   In the moonshine where he sat—

I heard the midnight clocks all round,
   In distant falls and swells—
I heard a little silver sound,
   The clink of elfin bells—
But will my princess be unbound,
   If anybody tells?

        M

AUTUMN SONG

THE ash-berry clusters are darkly red;
  The leaves of the limes are almost shed;
The passion-flower hangs out her yellow fruit;
The sycamore puts on her brownest suit.

AUTUMN SONG

After a silence, the wind complains,
Like a creature longing to burst its chains;
The swallows are gone, I saw them gather,
I heard them murmuring of the weather.

The clouds move fast, the south is blowing,
The sun is slanting, the year is going;
O I love to walk where the leaves lie dead,
And hear them rustle beneath my tread!

THE DRUMMER-BOY AND THE
SHEPHERDESS

DRUMMER-BOY, drummer-boy, where is your
  drum?
And why do you weep, sitting here on your
  thumb?
The soldiers are out, and the fifes we can hear;
But where is the drum of the young grenadier?

"My dear little drum it was stolen away
Whilst I was asleep on a sunshiny day;
It was all through the drone of a big bumble-
    bee,
And sheep and a shepherdess under a tree."

Shepherdess, shepherdess, where is your crook?
And why is your little lamb over the brook?
It bleats for its dam, and dog Tray is not by,
So why do you stand with a tear in your eye?

"My dear little crook it was stolen away
Whilst I dreamt a dream on a morning in May;
It was all through the drone of a big bumble-
    bee,
And a drum and a drummer-boy under a tree."

LULLABY

THE wind whistled loud at the window-pane—
   Go away, wind, and let me sleep!
Ruffle the green grass billowy plain,
   Ruffle the billowy deep!
"Hush-a-bye, hush! the wind is fled,
The wind cannot ruffle the soft smooth bed,—
   Hush thee, darling, sleep!"

LULLABY

The ivy tapped at the window-pane,—
   Silence, ivy! and let me sleep!
Why do you patter like drops of rain,
   And then play creepity-creep?
"Hush-a-bye, hush! the leaves shall lie still,
The moon is walking over the hill,—
   Hush thee, darling, sleep!"

A dream-show rode in on a moonbeam white,—
   Go away, dreams, and let me sleep!
The show may be gay and golden bright,
   But I do not care to peep.
"Hush-a-bye, hush! the dream is fled,
A shining angel guards the bed,
   Hush thee, darling, sleep!"

CLEAN CLARA

WHAT! not know our Clean Clara?
    Why, the hot folks in Sahara,
And the cold Esquimaux,
Our little Clara know!
Clean Clara, the Poet sings,
Cleaned a hundred thousand things!

CLEAN CLARA

She cleaned the keys of the harpsichord,
She cleaned the hilt of the family sword,
She cleaned my lady, she cleaned my lord;
All the pictures in their frames,
Knights with daggers, and stomachered dames—
Cecils, Godfreys, Montforts, Græmes,
Winifreds—all those nice old names!

She cleaned the works of the eight-day clock,
She cleaned the spring of a secret lock,
She cleaned the mirror, she cleaned the cupboard;
All the books she India-rubbered!

She cleaned the Dutch-tiles in the place,
She cleaned some very old-fashioned lace;
The Countess of Miniver came to her,
"Pray, my dear, will you clean my fur?"
All her cleanings are admirable;

To count your teeth you will be able,
If you look in the walnut table!

She cleaned the tent-stitch and the sampler;
She cleaned the tapestry, which was ampler;
Joseph going down into the pit,
And the Shunammite woman with the boy in a
    fit;

You saw the reapers, *not* in the distance,
And Elisha coming to the child's assistance,
With the house on the wall that was built for
   the prophet,
The chair, the bed, and the bolster of it;

The eyebrows all had a twirl reflective,
Just like an eel; to spare invective,
There was plenty of colour, but no perspective.
However, Clara cleaned it all,
With a curious lamp, that hangs in the hall!
She cleaned the drops of the chandeliers,—
Madame in mittens was moved to tears!

She cleaned the cage of the cockatoo,
The oldest bird that ever grew;
I should say a thousand years old would do—
I'm sure he looked it; but nobody knew;
She cleaned the china, she cleaned the delf,
She cleaned the baby, she cleaned herself!

To-morrow morning she means to try
To clean the cobwebs from the sky;
Some people say the girl will rue it,
But my belief is she will do it.

So I've made up my mind to be there to see:
There's a beautiful place in the walnut-tree;
The bough is as firm as the solid rock;
She brings out her broom at six o'clock.

THE LAVENDER BEDS

THE garden was pleasant with old-fashioned
 flowers,
The sunflowers and hollyhocks stood up like
 towers ;
There were dark turncap lilies and jessamine rare,
And sweet thyme and marjoram scented the air.

THE LAVENDER BEDS

The moon made the sun-dial tell the time wrong;
'Twas too late in the year for the nightingale's
 song;
The box-trees were clipped, and the alleys were
 straight,
Till you came to the shrubbery hard by the gate.

The fairies stepped out of the lavender beds,
With mob-caps, or wigs, on their quaint little
 heads;
My lord had a sword and my lady a fan;
The music struck up and the dancing began.

I watched them go through with a grave minuet;
Wherever they footed the dew was not wet;
They bowed and they curtsied, the brave and the
 fair;
And laughter like chirping of crickets was there.

Then all on a sudden a church clock struck loud:
A flutter, a shiver, was seen in the crowd,
The cock crew, the wind woke, the trees tossed
 their heads,
And the fairy folk hid in the lavender beds.

Little Ditties.

LITTLE DITTIES

I

WINIFRED WATERS sat and sighed
   Under a weeping willow;
When she went to bed she cried,
  Wetting all the pillow;

Kept on crying night and day,
  Till her friends lost patience;
"What shall we do to stop her, pray?"
  So said her relations.

Send her to the sandy plains,
  In the zone called torrid:
Send her where it never rains,
  Where the heat is horrid!

Mind that she has only flour
   For her daily feeding ;
Let her have a page an hour
   Of the driest reading,—

Navigation, logarithm,
   All that kind of knowledge,—
Ancient pedigrees go with 'em,
   From the Heralds' College.

When the poor girl has endured
   Six months of this drying,
Winifred will come back cured,
   Let us hope, of crying.

Then she will not day by day
   Make those mournful faces,
And we shall not have to say,
   " Wring her pillow-cases."

II

THERE was a Little Boy, with two little eyes,
And he had a little head that was just the proper
size,
And two little arms, and two little hands;
On two little legs this Little Boy he stands.

Now, this Little Boy would now and then be cross
Because that he could only be the very thing he
was;
He wanted to be this, and then he wanted to be
that;
His head was full of wishes underneath his little
hat!

" I wish I was a drummer to beat a kettledrum,
I wish I was a giant to say Fee-fo-fi-faw-fum :
I wish I was a captain to go sailing in a ship ;
I wish I was a huntsman to crack a nice whip.

I wish I was a horse to go sixty miles an hour ;
I wish I was the man that lives up in the light-
    house tower ;
I wish I was a sea-gull with two long wings ;
I wish I was a traveller to see all sorts of things.

I wish I was a carpenter ; I wish I was a lord ;
I wish I was a soldier, with a pistol and a sword ;
I wish I was the man that goes up high in a
    balloon ;
I wish, I wish, I wish I could be something else,
    and soon !"

But all the wishing in the world is not a bit of
    use ;
That Little Boy this very day he stands in his
    own shoes ;
That Little Boy is still but little Master What-do-
    you-call,
As much as if that Little Boy had never wished
    at all !

He eats his bread and butter, and he likes it very
    much ;

He grubs about, and bumps his head, and bowls
    his hoop, and such ;

And his father and his mother they say, " Thank
    the gracious powers,

Those wishes cannot wish away that Little Boy of
    ours ! "

III

Godfrey Gordon Gustavus Gore—
No doubt you have heard the name before—
Was a boy who never would shut a door!

The wind might whistle, the wind might roar,
And teeth be aching and throats be sore,
But still he never would shut the door.

His father would beg, his mother implore,
"Godfrey Gordon Gustavus Gore,
We really *do* wish you would shut the door!"

LITTLE DITTIES

Their hands they wrung, their hair they tore ;
But Godfrey Gordon Gustavus Gore
Was deaf as the buoy out at the Nore.

When he walked forth the folks would roar,
" Godfrey Gordon Gustavus Gore,
Why don't you think to shut the door?"

They rigged out a Shutter with sail and oar,
And threatened to pack off Gustavus Gore
On a voyage of penance to Singapore.

But he begged for mercy, and said, " No more !
Pray do not send me to Singapore
On a Shutter, and then I will shut the door!"

" You will?" said his parents ; "then keep on
    shore !
But mind you do ! For the plague is sore
Of a fellow that never will shut the door,
Godfrey Gordon Gustavus Gore !"

IV

Timothy Tight, Timothy Tight,
Says he will neither have sup nor bite,
Nor comb to his hair, nor sleep in his bed,
Till he has done what he thinks in his head.

LITTLE DITTIES

What is it poor little Timothy thinks
To do before he eats, or drinks,
Or combs, or sleeps? Why, Timothy Tight
Thinks in his head to turn black into white!

He caught a crow, and he tried with that,
He tried again with a great black cat,
He tried again with dyes and inks;
He keeps on trying to do what he thinks!

He tried with lumps of coals a score,
He tried with jet, and a blackamoor,
He tried with these till he got vext—
He means to try the Black Sea next.

V

Baby, baby, bless her;
How shall mammy dress her?

The summer cloud
Is not too proud
To find soft wool to dress her.

The bluebell
Is a true bell,
And will find the blue to dress her.

205

The cherry-tree
Is a merry tree,
And will find the pink to dress her.

The lily bright
Will find the white,
The beautiful white to dress her.

The leaves in the wood
Are sweet and good,
And will find the green to dress her.

The honeysuckle,
With buds for a buckle,
Will make a girdle to dress her.

The heavens hold
Both silver and gold
In the stars, and they will dress her.

VI

THERE was a man so very tall,
That when you spoke you had to bawl
Through both your hands, put like a cup,
His head was such a long way up !

But there was something even sadder,—
His wife had to go up a ladder
Whenever she desired a kiss—
And he, alas, was proud of this !

Said he, " I am the tallest man
That ever grew since time began,"
As down on a house-top he sat ;
Well, he *was* tall ; but what of that ?

This monstrous man, as we shall see,
Was punished for his vanity :
He grew and grew,—the people placed
A telescope to see his waist!

He grew and grew—you could not see
Without a telescope his knee ;
He grew till he was over-grown,
And seen by over-sight alone !

VII

My man John
To sea is gone
All in a wicker cradle;
The cradle creaks,
The cradle leaks,
But John has got a ladle.

VIII

THERE is a curious boy, whose name
    Is Lumpy Loggerhead;
His greatest joy is—oh, for shame!—
    To spend his time in bed.

211

They fit with gongs alarum clocks
  That make your blood run chill;
And they encourage crowing cocks
  Beneath his window-sill.

In vain the gongs,—his eyes are shut —
  In vain the cocks do crow;
Empty on him a water-butt,
  And he will say, " Hallo ! "

But only in a drowsy style,
  And in a second more
He sleeps—and, oh ! to see him smile !
  And, oh ! to hear him snore !

He seems to carry, all day long,
  Sleep in his very shape;
And, though you may be brisk and strong,
  You often want to gape

When Lumpy Loggerhead comes near,
  Whose bed is all his joy.
How glad I am he is not here,
  That very sleepy boy !

IX

THERE was a giant walked out one day,
To eat whatever came in his way;
This giant was greedy, this giant was grim,
And the people were all afraid of him.

He crossed the field and came into the street,
And a dainty damsel he there did meet;
"What is your name?" says he to her,
And she says, "Lucy Locket, sir."

"A very nice name is Lucy Locket,
And you will just fit my waistcoat-pocket;"
So said the giant, and popped her in,
And the pocket was more than up to her chin.

The giant says, "Oh, this is the street;
Your father and mother I mean to eat."
But Lucy, she thought, "You wicked man!"
And then to tickle him she began.

Her hand was light, her hand was small,
He scarcely felt it at first at all;
She tickled and tickled, and by degrees
He felt as if he should like to sneeze!

This giant could growl, and shout, and roar,
But he never had laughed in his life before,
And now he began to look less grim
As Lucy kept on tickling him.

The people heard and the people saw,—
"He, hee!" says the giant, "ha hah! haw haw!"
Oh, they were puzzled, but Lucy Locket
Made signs to them out of his doublet-pocket.

His mad guffaws for a mile they hear,
His mouth is stretched from ear to ear;
Thinks he, "To laugh is a pleasant plan,
So now I will laugh as long as I can."

He laughed till he ached and his eyes grew dim,
As Lucy kept on tickling him;
He laughed till the tears ran down his face,
And he fell down, flop, in the market-place!

Then out of his pocket Lucy leapt,
And close behind him the people crept;
With twisted cables and iron bands
And things of that sort they tied his hands.

They tied his hands and they tied his feet,
They said, "Pray, what would you like to eat?"
And Lucy got into his pocket again,
And made him laugh like a thousand men!

He laughed all day, he laughed all night,
He laughed when they woke in the morning
  light,
He laughed that week and the fortnight after,—
Travellers came to hear his laughter!

They let him laugh on to his heart's content
In a show as high as the Monument;
They gave to Lucy a penny clear
For every person who came to hear,
So now the girl is as rich as a prince,
For he has been laughing ever since.

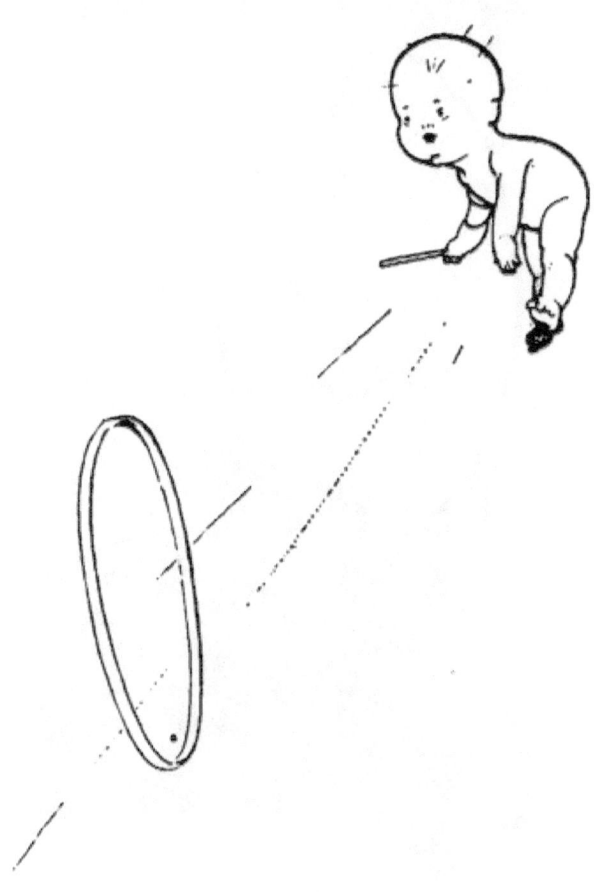

X

Baby, baby bowling,
Set the hoop a-rolling;
　The hoop will wait
　At the turnpike gate,
And the man will take the toll in.

217

XI

Diddy Doddy Dumpling,
Muslin all a-crumpling;
Cap like an arch,
Stiff with starch—
Diddy Doddy Dumpling!

218

LITTLE DITTIES

Niddy Noddy Nursey,
How shall we make *her* see ?
  Bobs and blinks,
   Wobbles and winks—
Niddy Noddy Nursey !

XII

What do you think?
Why, pen and ink,
And a rosewood desk, or better;
The old black hen,
She mended the pen,
And the little pig wrote a letter.

XIII

JOHNNY drew a picture, but Johnny couldn't
    spell;
What he wrote under it I'm ashamed to tell;
All in large capitals Johnny wrote PECTURE,
Stuck it up upon the wall, and said that he
    would lecture;
What a funny lecture, though, Johnny will
    deliver;
While, with aches at his mistakes, all the people
    shiver!

XIV

Mind the cat,
Find the cat,
Who will be first behind the cat?
The cat's on the mat
In a billycock hat,
And that's the way to find the cat.

XV

Large eyes, little eyes, brown eyes, blue eyes,
My doll has had an accident and wants a pair of
  new eyes;
Strong legs, long legs, one leg and two legs,
My doll has had an accident and wants a pair of
  new legs;
Dribble dribble, trickle trickle, what a lot of raw
  dust!
Dolly had an accident, and out came the sawdust!

XVI

One, two, three,
Put the cups for tea;
Two, three, one,
Toast a Sally-Lunn.
Fanny sat down
In a new gown;
Emma spilt the milk
Over the satin and silk,
One, two, three,
" Never wear silk at tea,"

(Two, three, one),
So said Dimity Dunn;
Ever so many slices,
Bread and butter, and niceys;
One, two, three,
White sugar for me!
Two, three, one,
Now the tea's done.

XVII

Baby has just been feeding;
  See, he has emptied the cup!
And now he sits a-reading,
  But the book is wrong-side up;

226

Will he make out what the book is about
  Before it is time to sup?
    His fist he doubles;
    He blows little bubbles;
    He splutters and stutters,
    And tells you his troubles,
Reading the book that is wrong-side up!

XVIII

" Daughter, daughter,
Mind the water!"
   She said she never should,
So she went in
Right up to her chin,
   And did not find it good;

For the water was bitter,
And made her twitter,
   As nobody thought she could !
She cried in haste,
   " What a nasty taste !
   I wish I had understood ! "

Oh, send and save her !
A beautiful flavour
   Is not to be found in the flood ;
And wine or tea
Is the drink for me
   At a picnic in the wood !

XIX

Hurly Burly
And Curly Wurly
 Went to the fair together;
It rained in the night
For more delight,
 And it was windy weather.

Hurly Burly jumped the stiles,
  Laughed and in-and-outed;
Hurly Burly ran for miles,
  Hurly Burly shouted.

Curly Wurly went off in smiles,
  Except just when she pouted!
The Quakeress peeped from under the tiles,
  Saying, "If I could smile as thou did!"

Hurly Burly's talk was mad,
  Like Singlestick and Latin;
Curly Wurly a sweet tongue had,
  And she was soft as satin.

Then Hurly Burly and Curly Wurly,
  When they had their airing,
Came home betimes, like a poet's rhymes,
  Each of them with a fairing.

For he had a monstrous popgun got,
  That went with a noise like thunder;
And she had a beautiful true-love knot,
  That never would come in sunder.

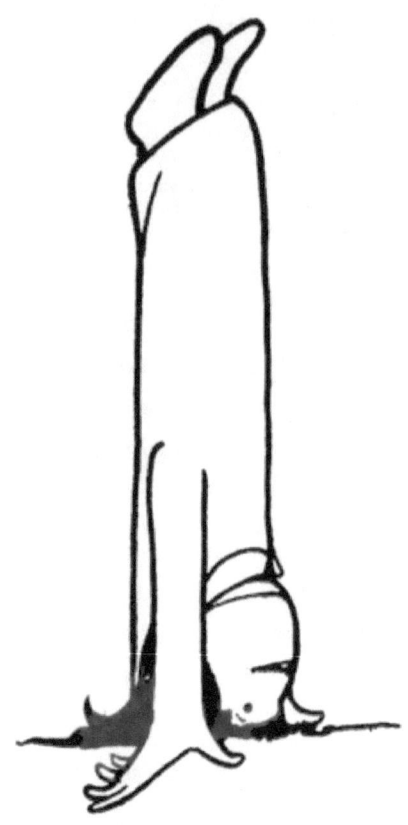

XX

NATHAN NOBB,
Oh, what a job!
Always walked on his head;
His mother would sob
To his brother Bob,
And his father took to his bed.

They made him a boot
His head to suit,
But a horrible thing must be said,—
His hair took root,
And began to shoot,
One day, in the garden bed!

So there he stands
With the help of his hands
And a little support from his nose:
The gardener man,
With the watering-can,
Says, "Gracious, how fast he grows!"

XXI

Blow, blow, east wind!
   What does the east wind do?
Shine, shine, sunlight!
   And what does the sunshine do?

The sunshine clear
Goes there and here,
   And searches in every nook,
And, while it is going,
The wind is blowing
   Farther than you can look ;
The east wind blows,
It sweeps, it goes
   The whole world through ;
As the world grows green,
It sweeps it clean,
   And the sky is a pale, cold blue :
Blow, blow, east wind,
   Finish your blowing, do !
And the west wind, dear, will soon be here,
   With skies of deep, warm blue.

Baby's Bell

BABY'S' BELLS

I

DING, Dong, and Dell
    Went and sat under the bell,
Saying, "Bell, bell, bell,
What have you got to tell?"
And the clapper rose and fell,
And the bell rang well
Over Ding, Dong, and Dell,
As they sat under the bell.

BABY'S BELLS

Here is pencil, and here is pen,
Walk up, ladies and gentlemen!
Here are their pictures, as you see,
Ding, and Dong, and Dell make three,
There they are, and here are we.

First there is Ding, a dot of a thing,
And, not to go wrong, her brother Dong,
A little older and ever so much bolder,
And both of them seem ready to sing,
And Dell will belong and take part in the song.

Now Dell—I am not so sure about Dell—
Dell wears a mask, and hides till you ask,
And peeps at you from over a screen;
But if you must know the truth of it,—well!—
I really am not so sure about Dell.

So Ding, Dong, and Dell
Went and sat under the bell,
Saying, " Bell, bell, bell,
What have you got to tell?"
And the clapper rose and fell,
And the bell rang well
Over Ding, Dong, and Dell,
As they sat under the bell.

II

Ding and Dong went out a-walking,
Ding and Dong were gaily talking:
"My eyes are strong,
You know," says Dong,
"And once on a time I saw through a wall."
"And so did I," says little Ding,
"I also can do a wonderful thing."

Thus they disputed, and by-and-bye
Poor little Ding began to cry.
"You didn't," says Dong; "it isn't true——"
I did, you didn't, no more did you,
You didn't, I did, you didn't, pooh!

So they came squabbling to Dell, who said,
"You both deserve to be put to bed.
When Ding saw through a wall, the wall
Was made of glass, and that is all!
When Dong saw through a wall, it had
A hole in it." Then both were glad,
Ding and Dong, that they thought to ask
Dell of the screen, who wore the mask;
And Ding and Dong said, "Clever Dell;
Who would have thought that Dell could tell?

III

Ding and Dong, because they find
   Dell so very clever,
Say they have made up their mind
   To go in masks for ever.
Is there wisdom in a mask?
   They are none the wittier yet;
Is there beauty? do not ask!
   They are none the prettier yet!

IV

Tʜᴇ girls and the boys
They made such a noise
At play, that they frightened away their toys.
Dolly, she fled,
And went to bed,
Because she had caught such a pain in her head!

The German bricks,
The candlesticks,
The elephant,
And the cormorant,
The ass and the horse,
And the rest in their course,
(But there was no shark,)
Of the Noah's Ark,
The saucers and the cups,
And the little woolly pups,
(You heard them bark)
Belonging to the Ark,
Were frightened, like all the rest of the toys,
And hid themselves from the dreadful noise:
So, if I were you, next time I played,
I would not be so loud in the noise that I made!

V

SPARROW, sparrow,
Swift as an arrow,
What are you doing there in the sun?
A hunter am I,
And the white butterfly
I am chasing to-day in the summer sun.

VI

Sɪᴛ in the sun
Till the day is done,
Reading and working and making fun:
Then look at the moon,
And eat with a spoon
A basin of sop that is made from a bun.

217

VII

WHAT makes the starling so merry?
The starling has had a cherry,
A cherry as soft as a baby's cheek,
I can see the pulp hanging out of his beak.
This is the lass, this is the lad,
That like to see the starling glad!

248

VIII

Here is a rug
That looks very snug;
And here is a cat—
What shall we be at?
You take off your bonnet,
I take off my hat,
And let us sit upon it,
And talk to the cat—
Not upon the hat, you know,
But on the little rug—
The hat would not come pat, you know,
But, oh, the rug is snug!

BABY'S BELLS

Ding, Dong, Dell,
Said " Bell, bell, bell!
What have you got to tell?"—
And you hear what the bells say
From Greenwich up to Chelsea;
Ring, ring, ring,
About this, and the other thing,
These, and those, and that,
The cat, and the rug, and the mat,
The Noah's Ark and the sparrow,
And the sop as soft as marrow!
And whether you live by Bow bells,
Or out in a place with no bells,
And neither at Greenwich nor at Chelsea,
You shall hear what the different bells say
From Ding, Dong, and Dell,
Who like to sit under the bell.

Said Ding, Dong, and Dell,
" Listen to the bell!"
Now it was not bell, but bells,
For the bells that rang were many,—
Bells upon bells ;
You shall have a silver penny,
Or almost anything else,
If you can count the bells
That are ringing.   And what for ?—
Ding, Dong, and Dell
Will explain every bell,
That is to say, the bells,
Neither less nor more
Than the meaning of the Bells.

X

"Who are you?"
Says One to Two;
Says Two to One "I'm plenty;"
"Think again!"
Says little Ten,
And, "Think again!" says Twenty.

XI

LILY white, Rose red,
Standing in the garden-bed;
Wind from the south, wind from the west,
Can you tell me which is best?

XII

JOHNNY has finished his lessons,
　All in good time;
Then in his very　resence,
　The bells set up a chime;

All round the school-room
　The bells began to ring,
All round the school-room,
　"Johnny is a king!"

XIII

Now, then, let us tell a tale—
Six travellers in a dale,
Feeling weak about the knees,
Resting under six elm-trees;
Six robbers, after them,
Draw their swords and say, "Ahem!"
Then the travellers, who have not
Any weapons with them got,
Shake and shiver in their boots,
And they play upon their flutes
Then the robbers six remark
To the travellers, "It is dark."

"No," say they, "it is not quite. —
Every traveller strikes a light !
"Will you see some conjuring tricks?"
"Yes," say all the robbers six ;
Then six tigers and six lions
Came along and roared defiance,
And the thieves and travellers too
Could not tell what next to do :
"This," said they, "is very sad!"
Then there came an earthquake bad,
And the air was very hot,
And it swallowed up the lot.

XIV

WHEN Ding and Dong,
    Had finished a song,
One day, they went to Dell,
    And to him or her
    Said, " We should prefer
That you should do something as well,—
    Something amusing
    Of your own choosing."—
" And so I will," says Dell.

    There goes a bell,
    Ding, dong, dell,
    A cracked old bell,
    A shaky old bell,
    A quavering old bell,—
    Can anybody tell
    What the cracked old bell is saying?

BABY'S BELLS

"Yes, I can tell," says Dell,
" Without measuring or weighing,
And this is what it is saying;
Ding, dong, dell!
Goes the cracked old bell;
And this is what it is saying :

" There is an old woman whose name it is Gray,
Lives in an old town in an old-fashioned way;
You cross an old bridge, and go up an old road,
And down an old lane, to find out her abode.

" She wears an old cap that stands ever so high;
She looks through old goggles as round as the
  sky;
She keeps an old dog, and a very old cat;
She sits in an arm-chair much older than that.

" She crosses her old arms; she shakes her old
  pate;
She only hears half of the tale you relate;
She puts her old ear-trumpet up, and cries
  'What?'
And when you say 'Freezing!' she thinks you
  say 'Hot!'

259

' She thinks as she sits that she hears a bell
  ring,
As even and slow as a rook on the wing;
It booms in her old ear; she shakes her old
  head;
That old bell says, *Put out the lights and to bed!*"

XV

DING, dong, dell,
Bell, bell, bell!
What have you got to tell?
What is it the bells say,
From Greenwich up to Chelsea,—
The bells of wandering fancies,
  Up and down
  By sea and town
Like knights in old romances?
What is it that the bells say?
What is it you hear Dell say?
Explaining what the bells say?

BABY'S BELLS

An August day: an August night;
  A morning in September;
A lily red; a jasmine white;
  What more do you remember?

A harvest-moon, a hunter's moon;
  A partridge on the moorland;
A stack of wheat: an afternoon
  In a yacht out by the Foreland.

A foxglove faded, a brook to be waded,
  Apples and pears grown redder;
And the ways of the birds, which, without any
      words,
  Say, "Come let us consider!"

XVI

THEN those bells stop,
The bells of wandering fancies
And Autumn and Summer chances;
263

BABY'S BELLS

And a bell rings with a flop,
A sort of heavy drop,
A distant blunt bark,
As if it was made in the dark,
And lived underground like a mole,
And the rope was as black as a coal.
O bell, what a comical voice!
What a stupid sort of noise!
Do you call it ringing or drumming?
And who is it that is coming?
It must be a bogie of some sort,
A blunt, black, stupid, dumb sort!
Hark! what do we hear this bell say?
And what do you hear Dell say?

"This is the King of the Blackaways,
   And very black is he,
So black you cannot see his face,—
   Not you! No more can we!

    Black, black,
    Breast and back;
    Teeth and eyes,
    Lips likewise;
    Just like a blot
    Tied in a knot!

And oh, the land of the Blackaways,
Where this King reigns, is a very black place.

BABY'S BELLS

The grass is black, and so are the trees,
The chalk is black, and so are the geese:
The milk, the eggs, the flour, and the cheese;
The sheets and the shirts; for it all agrees!"

Get you gone, Blackaway King, if you please!
And dine off black bread, and flesh of black
    geese,
Where the grass grows black on the Blackaway
    leas!

XVII

WHAT sort of bell is this?
A wisdom bell,
Or a nonsense bell?
What sort of bell is this?

266

"Bell, bell, how high do you hang?"
I said to the bell as it rang, as it rang,
And "Never *you* mind!" a goblin sang,
One who did dwell
Within the bell!
Wibbling-wobbling
Went the bell,
And what had the goblin
Got to tell?
Why, ill said or well said,
This is what the bell said;
Wisdom bell
Or nonsense bell,
This is what the bell said:

BETSY BOUNCE—her taste was such—
Of her bonnet thought too much;
Strutting up and down she went,
(People wondered what she meant).

In the villages and towns
Folks said, "Look how Betsy Bounce
Takes her walks around the nation!"
She thought this was admiration.

"Oh, that all the world," says she,
"Could my lovely bonnet see,

BABY'S BELLS

See my bonnet, but without
All this walking round about!"

For in truth the girl got tired,
Though her bonnet was admired,
Of this walking round the nation
After people's admiration.

Now observe what came to pass—
One fine day this foolish lass
Found her bonnet growing, growing
On her head like flowers a-blowing!

Higher still, and higher piled
Grew the bonnet on the child,
Farther back and farther out,
Farther down and round about!

Rivers sprawling to the sea
Both the strings appeared to be,
Till the bow beneath her chin
Shut her up and shut her in.

Oh, how foreigners did stare
When her bonnet filled the air,
Russian, Turk, and Mexican,
Folks in India and Japan!

BABY'S BELLS

Betsy Bounce has her desire :
All the world can now admire !
Yet perhaps she will not pout
When the bonnet is worn out.

But her parents, being poor,
Cannot, for a time, procure
Betsy Bounce another hat,
So she must keep on with that.

XVIII

You cannot count the bluebells
  That are upon the heath,—
The ferns stand tall and stately,
  The bells hang underneath:
But I can count the tassels
  As big as flowers of clover
That hang on baby's curtain,
  The curtain that hangs over:
And when I rock the cradle
  The tassels swing and swing,
And they make fairy music,
  And baby hears them ring:
Ding-dong in the morning,
  And in the evening too,
Rhime, chime, in fairy time,
  Baby, dear, for you!

XIX

WHEN the moon was on the wane,
Ding was looking through the window-pane,
Dong was counting drops of rain,
And Dell was thinking with might and main;
But all of them listened to the bell again,
A wisdom bell,
Or a nonsense bell?

271

And the goblin said, " Let Dell explain,
She knows what the bells say
From Greenwich up to Chelsea,
She will explain what the bells say!"

XX

O HAVE you heard of Reuben Rammer,
The little fellow that *would* stammer?
He talked at such a headlong rate
That at last he got through Stuttering Gate.

273

BABY'S BELLS

If fellows will talk madly fast,
They come to Stuttering Gate at last;
Some boys take warning and they pause,—
Not thus with Reuben Rammer 'twas.

He made a plunge, dashed past the bar.
He went on stuttering fast and far;
And what was the result? Why, now
He speaks no better than a cow!

He has been trying,—how absurd!—
For several months to speak a word;
His mouth works open like a door,
His arm goes like a semaphore!

He strives to say what he desires;
His jaws jolt up like jaws on wires;
But Reuben Rammer could not speak
When last I saw him this day week!

How awkward to be driven to use
A pencil to express your views,
Try to say, "Hallo, Johnny Brown!"
And yet be forced to write it down!

XXI

Wᴀᴇɴ the bell sounds
    Over land and sea,
And the wind, in its rounds,
    Blowing fresh and free,
Carries the ringing
    Far out of sight,
There where the clinging
    Sails are white,
White on the sea;
    And over the hills.

275

BABY'S BELLS

How far does the sound
  Of the sweet bell go?
Over the round
  Where the waters flow,
And up to the bound
  Where the winds can blow.
Is it lost, is it found,
  Is it gone, do you know?

Nonsense Rhyme

NONSENSE RHYMES

TUESDAY

CARRY and Kate
    Swallowed a slate:
David and Dick
Lived in a stick:
Hetty and Helen
Said, "Oh, what a dwelling!"

TUESDAY

Patty and Prue
Took baths in a flue :
Nathan and Ned
Caught fish in their bed :
Nothing could hide 'em,
And Dorothy fried 'em :
This was on Tuesday,
Which always was news day.

JOLLY JACK

" IF black was white,
    And white was black,
I would swallow a light
    And live in a sack,
And swim on a kite,"—
    Says jolly Jack.

281

THE DUCK AND HER DUCKLINGS

THERE was an old duck which had three
little ducks,
Three little ducklings, chuck, chuck, chucks!
  She took them for a walk,
    And she march'd them back,
  And taught them how to say,
    "Quack, quack, quack!"

The ducklings went behind, and the duck went
before,
Three ducks and one duck, that made four:

282

DUCK AND HER DUCKLINGS

A duckling is a duck, if I know white from
black,
But a duck is not a duckling, though,
"Quack, quack, quack!"

This duck was genteel, and she walk'd with great
state,
Then cried, "Now, ducklings, mark my gait,
So much, you see, depends on the style of
the back;"
And the ducklings said, "Yes, mamma,
Quack, quack, quack!"

LITTLE BEN BUTE

O LITTLE Ben Bute
    Had a flute, flute, flute,
And went about the world in a knickerbocker
        suit;
    Down, up and down,
    And round about the town,
He played and he played tootle-too, toot, toot!
    Tootle-too, tootle-too-ey!

He could not play it well,
So the notes rose and fell,
Tootle, tootle-too, with a twirl and a squeak;
The wind, puff, puff,
Was forty times enough,
That he sent into the flute from his cheek, cheek,
cheek,
Tootle-too, tootle-too-ey!

Then people to the lad
"Said, "This is very bad!
Our ears they are splitting, with your toot, toot,
toot;
Is there no one within reach—
What, no one!—who will teach
Little Bute how to play upon the flute, flute,
flute?"
Tootle-too, tootle-too-ey!

THE DREAM OF A GIRL WHO LIVED
AT SEVEN-OAKS

SEVEN sweet singing birds up in a tree;
   Seven swift sailing-ships white upon the
  sea;
Seven bright weather-cocks shining in the sun;
Seven slim race-horses ready for a run;
Seven gold butterflies, flitting overhead;
Seven red roses blowing in a garden bed;
Seven white lilies, with honey bees inside them;
Seven round rainbows with clouds to divide them;
Seven pretty little girls with sugar on their lips;
Seven witty little boys, whom everybody tips;
Seven nice fathers, to call little maids joys;
Seven nice mothers, to kiss the little boys;
Seven nights running I dreamt it all plain;
With bread and jam for supper I could dream it
  all again!

THE DREAM OF A BOY WHO LIVED
AT NINE-ELMS

NINE grenadiers, with bayonets in their guns;
   Nine bakers' baskets, with hot cross-buns;
Nine brown elephants, standing in a row;
Nine new velocipedes, good ones to go;
Nine knickerbocker suits, with buttons all com-
   plete;
Nine pair of skates with straps for the feet;

DREAM OF A BOY AT NINE-ELMS

Nine clever conjurors eating hot coals;
Nine sturdy mountaineers leaping on their poles;
Nine little drummer-boys beating on their drums;
Nine fat aldermen sitting on their thumbs;
Nine new knockers to our front door;
Nine new neighbours that I never saw before;
Nine times running I dreamt it all plain;
With bread and cheese for supper I could dream
   it all again!

FOUR LITTLE HISTORIES

I

THERE was an old man, and he had an old gun,
And he went to a cake shop, and aimed at a bun;
The bullet it shot the old baker's old cat,
"Stop thief!" says the baker, "why, what are you at?"

II

Jack and Joe were tinmen,
    And oh, but they were thin men!
    Bags of bones,
Or bags of stones,—
I think they couldn't have *been* men!

III

Sarah Page,
In a rage,
Drest in satin;
Bertha Newry,
Learning Latin,
In a fury,

FOUR LITTLE HISTORIES

Drest in silk,
And lapping milk—
Which is best? Oh, what a
  bother!
Neither one nor yet the other.

IV

Says Aleck to Alice,
"I live in a palace."
Says Alice to Tim,
"I don't believe him."
Says Tim to his cousin,
"I love you three dozen;"
The cousin, she wondered,
And asked for a hundred,
Instead of three dozen:
Says Tim, "You are fussing;
Three dozen I love you,
If that will not move you,
My love I will carry
To Magsie or Mary."

A BIG NOISE

TWENTY whales
    Lashing their tails;
Twenty guns
Fired at once;
Twenty cats
Howling in flats;
Twenty parrots
Calling carrots;
Twenty apiece,
Besides, of these,—
Lions roaring,
Giants snoring,
Waggons rolling,
Bells tolling;
These together,
In stormy weather,
With a steam hammer,
Would make a clamour.

THE ALARM

A GIANT at the door behind,
    For Baby? Nothing of the kind!
But even if a Giant were to come,
With an eye like an Orleans plum,
And hands like wolf's paws,
And teeth like horrible saws,
And a voice like a dreadful cough,
And he carried baby off,
And fed her up in a dungeon
(To fatten her for his luncheon),
A dungeon as high as the stars;
And, if the dungeon had bars,

And was guarded by a horrid vulture,
And an eagle of savage culture;
And if from the wall of the castle
A dragon hung like a tassel,
And the castle was built among mountains,
In a lonely situation
At the very end of creation,
With flames spouting round it like fountains—
Why, mother could find her way
To the castle any day,
And make the old dragon wriggle,
And fight the vulture and the eagle,
And blow up the castle—pop!
And bring baby home to her sop,
And the sop should have sugar extra,
Because the Giant had vexed her.

CICERO BRICK

I

THERE was a boy at Hampton Wick,
  Whose name, as it happened, was Cicero
Brick;
He fell in love in desperate fashion
With a girl who fully returned his passion.

CICERO BRICK

But she had a father who said, " No, no!
What! marry a boy named Cicero?
Never, with my consent, my dear!"—
What happened next we soon shall hear.

The daughter wept till the father said,
" Cicero Brick and you may wed
When he has spoken an oration
To an enormous congregation!"

II

The public felt no great surprise
When Cicero Brick did advertise
A course of lectures—five or six,—
O, what a notion of Cicero Brick's!

St. James's Hall, in Regent Street,
For these orations he said was meet;
The first oration that he spoke
Two dozen heard it—what a joke!

The next time ten, the next time four,
And then the public came no more;
But Cicero Brick—*this* who shall blame?—
Spoke the oration all the same.

"Read my advertisement," quoth he,
"And tell me what you in it see
About the oration's being *heard!*
It says, '*delivered.*' I keep my word!"

III

This was so honest and well-meant,
The father well-nigh did relent;
He said, "I never saw before
So persevering an orator!"

The lover spoke, perhaps with grace,
For two hours in that empty place!
The servants at the Hall let out
The fact, and it got noised about

At concerts, balls, and conversations,
That Cicero spoke these orations
In that huge Hall, week after week,
With no one there to hear him speak.

What was the consequence? A run,
A rush, to see and hear it done;
"We really *must* hear Cicero Brick!"
All London cried. The crowd was thick.

CICERO BRICK

They mobbed the men who took the pay;
Hundreds that night were turned away;
And Cicero Brick spoke this oration
To an enormous congregation!

The father of the girl he wooed
Now kept his promise, as he should;
The wedding feast of Cicero Brick
Came off at once near Hampton Wick;
And all the guests gave three cheers for
The persevering Orator.

THE OBSTINATE COW

THIS, if you please, is the Obstinate Cow,—
It all befell I will tell you how;
And that, if you please, is the Resolute Boy,—
He tugs at her tail, and he shouts, "Ahoy!"

It stands to reason, if you but think,
That the milk of an Obstinate Cow to drink
Must make a fellow grow obstinate—
There they are by the Manor-house gate.

THE OBSTINATE COW

He breakfasted, year after year,
On the milk of the cow that you see here;
Her name is Dapple, his name is Jim;
He pulls the cow, and the cow pulls him.

On the gate of the Manor-house may be read
That trespassers will be prosecuted;
The boy is right, and the cow is wrong,
But the cow, as it happens, is much more strong.

It *does* look awkward, and, if we attend,
We soon shall see how it all will end:
The Squire had a boy who was weak of bone,
And very much wanting in will of his own.

Admiring the pluck of Resolute Jim,
The Squire comes out, and he says to him,
" How came you so plucky?" and Jim says,
   " How?
I lived on the milk of this Obstinate Cow!"

" Oh, oh!" said the Squire, exceedingly pleased,
" Your father shall sell me this obstinate beast,
And you shall be cowherd."   So said, so done, —
The boy and his father enjoyed the fun.

THE OBSTINATE COW

The Squire's little boy, who was weak of bone,
And very much wanting in will of his own,
Was fed on the milk of the Obstinate Cow,
And, oh, what a change! You should see him
   now!

His mind is not worth a threepenny-bit,
'Tis dull as a ditch and as void of wit,
Yet he makes it up, and from day to day,
" *Do* change your mind!" the people say;
But his will is so strong that the people find
They cannot induce him to change his mind!

LAVENDER LADY

I

LIGHT Lady Lavender
Went to wed a Scavenger,
All the boys and girls in town
Laughed at Lady Lavender.

LAVENDER LADY

Light Lady Lavender
Hadn't any provender,
    All the boys and girls in town
Cried for Lady Lavender.

II

Lavender Lady got rich again,
And lived in a palace in Lavender Lane;
Flowers and provender!
Sweet Lady Lavender
Lived in a palace in Lavender Lane!

LAVENDER LADY

Lavender Lady is kind and gay,
Lavender House is not a long way;
  Puddings and pies,
  And turkeys' thighs,
And peacocks' tails, too, all over eyes!

Ask for her up, ask for her down,
If ever you go to London Town:
  In all the nation
  There's no relation
So kind as she is in London town!

III

"When you saw the New Moon pass"
   (Loud laughed the Scavenger),
"Did you look at her through glass,
   Proud Madam Lavender?"

LAVENDER LADY

"Stab my heart through with your horn!"
  Laughed Lady Lavender
To the New Moon all forlorn,
  Light Lady Lavender.

She fell sad, and he fell sick,
  Proud Lady Lavender.
O the snow fell fast and thick,
  Poor Lady Lavender!

"Take the broom and sweep the street,
  Proud Lady Lavender;"
O but she had dainty feet,
  Soft Lady Lavender.

"Sweep you must and sweep you shall,
  Soft Lady Lavender,
Up the Mall and down the Mall,
  Proud Lady Lavender.

"Have you done your sweeping yet,
  Proud Madam Scavenger?
Are your slippers cold and wet?"
  Poor Lady Lavender!

"Wet is wet, and cold is cold,"
  Wept Lady Lavender,
But the broom had turned to gold—
  Loud laughed the Scavenger

U

LAVENDER LADY

"Take your sampler, Madam Witch,
   Laid up in lavender;
Do you see a golden stitch,
   And a silver P in provender?"

Silver and gold for a golden broom,
   Rich Lady Lavender;
Then she danced all round the room,
   Light Lady Lavender.

Take the New Moon for a cup,
   Witch-lady Lavender;
Ladle the gold and silver up,
   Proud Lady Lavender.

"Here's an angel-piece for you,"
   Laughed Lady Lavender;
"Here's a golden guinea too,"
   Kind Lady Lavender!

Now we are all safe and sound
   (China plates and provender),
Now we're on Tom Tiddler's Ground,—
   Laugh, Lady Lavender!

ODD RHYMES

I

ROOK, rook,
   Read in a book!
Mouse, mouse,
Build a house!

311

ODD RHYMES

Bee, bee,
Get your tea!
Pig, pig,
Dance a jig!
Goose, goose,
Put on shoes!
Snail, snail,
Fill the pail!
Rabbit, rabbit,
Mind you stab it!
Cricket, cricket,
Mind you kick it!

II

My maid Molly,
  She pricked her thumb,
But only with holly,
  And the blood wouldn't come.

III

Martin, Martin
Went a carting;
And why did he travel?
To bring home some gravel.

IV

HEY-DOWN, high-down, furze and thistle,
Rain and wind, and a dog and whistle;
The wind blows, the rain drops,
The seeds are gone from the thistle-tops:
Whistle! find me a flower in the clover,
And you shall have turkey for supper, Rover!

315

TOPSYTURVEY-WORLD

IF the butterfly courted the bee,
  And the owl the porcupine;
If churches were built in the sea,
  And three times one was nine;
If the pony rode his master,
  If the buttercups ate the cows,
If the cat had the dire disaster
  To be worried, sir, by the mouse;

TOPSYTURVEY-WORLD

If mamma, sir, sold the baby
 To a gipsy for half-a-crown:
If a gentleman, sir, was a lady,—
 The world would be Upside-Down!

If any or all of these wonders
 Should ever come about,
I should not consider them blunders,
 For I should be Inside-Out!

Chorus: Ba-ba, black wool,
 Have you any sheep?
Yes, sir, a pack-full,
 Creep, mouse, creep!

317

TOPSYTURVEY-WORLD

Four-and-twenty little maids
   Hanging out the pie,
Out jumped the honey-pot,
   Guy-Fawkes, Guy!
Cross-latch, cross-latch,
   Sit and spin the fire,
When the pie was opened,
   The bird was on the brier!

MISS WAVER

L ITTLE Miss Waver
   Sings with a quaver,
A musical maid is she;
  Her voice is as clear
  As any you hear—
Let little Miss Waver be.

319

JEREMY JANGLE

J EREMY JANGLE
    Lives in a tangle;
You never know where to take him:
    His head is immense,
    And he might talk sense
Perhaps, if you could but make him.

JEREMY JANGLE

But he says that a tailor has a tail,
And every sailor is made for sale,
Also that bunting is made of buns!
But everybody can see at once
That this is nonsense. And yet his head
Is large, and he calls himself well read!

STALKY JACK

I KNEW a boy who took long walks,
   Who lived on beans, and ate the stalks;
To the Giants' Country he lost his way;
They kept him there for a year and a day.

STALKY JACK

But he has not been the same boy since;
An alteration he did evince;
For you may suppose that he underwent
A change in his notions of extent!

He looks with contempt on a nice high door,
And tries to walk in at the second floor!
He stares with surprise at a basin of soup,
He fancies a bowl as large as a hoop;
He calls the people minikin mites;
He calls a sirloin a couple of bites!
Things having come to these pretty passes,
They bought him some magnifying glasses.

He put on the goggles, and said, " My eyes!
The world has come to its proper size!"
But all the boys cry, "Stalky John!
There you go with your goggles on!"
What girl would marry him—and *quite* right --
To be taken for three times her proper height?
So this comes of taking extravagant walks,
And living on beans, and eating the stalks.

THE FIDDLER AND THE CROCODILE

ONE day a fiddler from the North,
   Out Memphis way, went walking forth;
He smoked his pipe and winked his lids,
And said, "Ah, ah! the Pyramids?"

FIDDLER AND THE CROCODILE

In this that fiddler took good heed;
The Pyramids were there indeed;
Sing Amon-Râ, sing Gizeh town,
Cheops, Cephrenes, mummy brown!

Thus said he on the banks of Nile,
When out there crawled a crocodile,
And when he turned, more scared than hurt,
The creature seized him by the skirt.

The crocodile was fierce and strong,
And twenty mortal feet was long.
The fiddler said, "It has been guessed
That music soothes the savage breast."

He drew his skirt—there being a pause—
From out the alligator's jaws;
For, crocodile or alligator,
The beast was something of that nature.

Sing bulrushes, sing cats and leeks,
Sing tawny gods with senseless beaks,
Sing scarabæi, if you've patience,
Isis, Osiris, inundations!

The fiddler raised his violin,
And to perform did next begin—
Sing lotus-flower, papyrus stiff,
Sarcophagus and hieroglyph!

FIDDLER AND THE CROCODILE

The district, since Amenophis,
Had never heard the like of this;
(Oh, to have seen the fiddler man
As up and down the scale he ran!)

That crocodile sat down to hear,
And to his eye there came a tear;
He turned it over in his mind;
His tail lay limp and long behind.

Affettuoso was the plan
Which struck at first that fiddler man;
Allegro next—his soul was stirr'd—
Con molto brio was the word.

At this the alligator brute—
Or crocodile, if that will suit—
Rose, much excited, from his seat,
And danced like mad, with heart and heat.

Sing Pompey, plectrum, strings and pegs,
Ichneumons, sand, and serpents' eggs,
Cheops, Cephrenes, Memnon, Sphinx—
" I *knew* it!"—so that fiddler thinks.

" I knew," said he, with joy and jest,
" That music soothes the savage breast;"
He swept the strings with maddening go,
From *presto* to *prestissimo*.

FIDDLER AND THE CROCODILE

But though the brute had dropped his plan
Of eating up at once the man,
It did not seem, his ways were such,
That music yet had soothed him much.

In fact he leapt and danced like mad;
He danced with all the legs he had;
Our friend, with violin to shoulder,
Sat, proudly playing, on a boulder.

He played until his arm grew weak,
And heat-drops gathered on his cheek;
He saw there would be mischief in it
If he but dropped his bow a minute!

For in that alligator's look
He read, as plain as in a book,
"Play on, or I will eat you yet,
With appetite the sharper set!"

Just as he thought he soon must faint
(And his emotions who can paint?)
He felt, and saw on looking round,
A curious trembling of the ground.

Thinks he, "This dancing crocodile
Is shaking up the land of Nile"—
He looked again, and saw, in places,
The pyramids leap from their bases!

327

FIDDLER AND THE CROCODILE

As six or seven together rushed,
He cried, "Confound it! I am crushed!"
But, happy chance! a moment later
They fell and crushed the alligator.

Sing Cleopatra's almond eye,
Sing reeds and hippopotami,
Sing tamarisk-trees by Mœris Lake,
And mud left in the sun to bake!

Then, as the fiddler wiped his brow,
Says he, "I feel exhausted now!"
Those ruins he no more regards
Than any fallen house of cards.

Out on the sands he chanced to find
A bit of temple to his mind,
And, as he sat down in the shade,
There came an Ethiop to his aid.

" De Hyksos," said that nigger lad,
" Dis way some secret cellarage had;
Yah, massa, yah, de best ob wine;
De Shepherd Kings, dey know'd de Rhine."

He quaffed those hocks, that fiddler bold,
Hocks five and thirty centuries old;
The cellar-man was older still—
Sing Typhon, Ptah, or what you will.

FIDDLER AND THE CROCODILE

Sing Ra, sing Sos, sing Seb, sing Khem,
Sing Mycerinus, after them;
Sing Diodorus Siculus,
Who tells untruths, for all his fuss;
Sing Manetho; but keep this clue —
The tale which *I* have told is true.

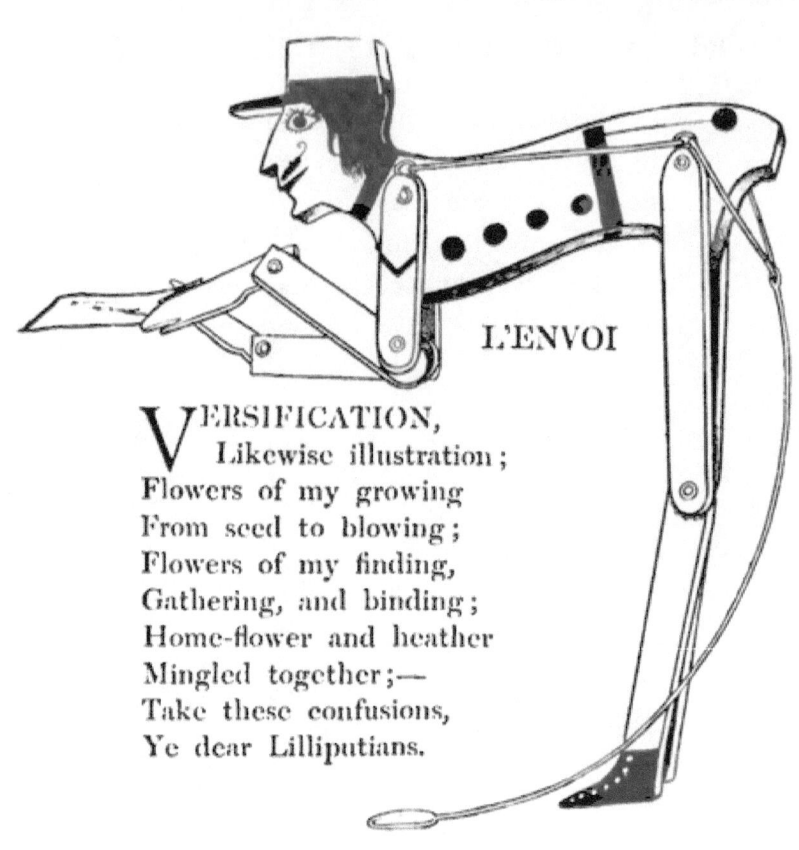

L'ENVOI

VERSIFICATION,
    Likewise illustration;
Flowers of my growing
From seed to blowing;
Flowers of my finding,
Gathering, and binding;
Home-flower and heather
Mingled together;—
Take these confusions,
Ye dear Lilliputians.

Printed by BALLANTYNE, HANSON & Co.
London & Edinburgh

www.ingramcontent.com/pod-product-compliance
Lightning Source LLC
Chambersburg PA
CBHW020807060726
47498CB00017B/907